WITCH SWITCH

Sibéal Pounder

Illustrated by
Laura Ellen Anderson

BLOOMSBURY
NEW YORK   LONDON   OXFORD   NEW DELHI   SYDNEY

First published in Great Britain in October 2015 by Bloomsbury Publishing Plc
Published in the United States of America in February 2017
by Bloomsbury Children's Books
www.bloomsbury.com

Bloomsbury is a registered trademark of Bloomsbury Publishing Plc

For information about permission to reproduce selections from this book, write to
Permissions, Bloomsbury Children's Books, 1385 Broadway, New York, New York 10018
Bloomsbury books may be purchased for business or promotional use. For information on
bulk purchases please contact Macmillan Corporate and Premium Sales Department at
specialmarkets@macmillan.com

Library of Congress Cataloging-in-Publication Data
Names: Pounder, Sibéal, author. | Anderson, Laura Ellen, illustrator.
Title: Witch switch / by Sibéal Pounder ; illustrated by Laura Ellen Anderson.
Description: New York : Bloomsbury, February 2017. | Series: Witch wars
Summary: Tiga Whicabim is settling in to the witchy, glitzy world of Ritzy City where
Peggy is Top Witch, but when Fran the Fabulous Fairy visits Linden House, the girls
realize that witches all across town are starting to disappear.
Identifiers: LCCN 2016023140 (print) • LCCN 2016045101 (e-book)
ISBN 978-1-61963-984-3 (hardcover) • ISBN 978-1-61963-985-0 (e-book)
Subjects: | CYAC: Witches—Fiction. | Fairies—Fiction. | Magic—Fiction. | Riddles—Fiction. |
Humorous stories. | BISAC: JUVENILE FICTION/Fantasy & Magic. |
JUVENILE FICTION/Humorous Stories. | JUVENILE FICTION/General.
Classification: LCC PZ7.1.P68 Wim 2017 (print) | LCC PZ7.1.P68 (e-book) | DDC[Fic]—dc23
LC record available at https://lccn.loc.gov/2016023140

Typeset by RefineCatch Limited, Bungay, Suffolk
Printed and bound in the U.S.A. by Berryville Graphics Inc., Berryville, Virginia
2 4 6 8 10 9 7 5 3 1

All papers used by Bloomsbury Publishing, Inc., are natural, recyclable products
made from wood grown in well-managed forests. The manufacturing processes
conform to the environmental regulations of the country of origin.

For Scullion —S. P.

For Aunty Kay —L. E. A.

SINKVILLE

THE COVES

PEARL PEAK

WAVELY WAY

THE SUNKEN SHIP ROAD SPA

PEARL PEAK ACADEMY

FOREST

LITTLE LEAF RESTAURANT

WHERE THE FIRST WITCH LANDED IN SINKVILLE
X

BROLLYWOOD

FAIRY TRAILER PARK

THE CAULDRON ISLANDS

BUBBLE BEACH

THE OLD CAULDRON FACTORY

THE TOWERS

WITCH SWITCH

The Story So Far

Last time in Ritzy City:

So you probably remember Fran the fairy zoomed up the sink pipes, told Tiga she was a witch, and then whisked her back down to the capital of Sinkville, Ritzy City, to compete in Witch Wars.

Tiga was delighted to be away from her evil guardian, Miss Heks, who is all kinds of terrible.

Before Witch Wars began, Tiga met Peggy, who promised to teach her some spells, and then they met Fluffanora, who at first seemed like she might be horrible but was in fact lovely.

Felicity Bat and Aggie Hoof, two complete witchy pains, were also competing and they

1

tried to knock Tiga out of the competition, and Peggy too, whom they called Piggy, which is just rude.

Fluffanora and fellow competitors Lizzie Beast, Patty Pigeon, Aggie Hoof, and twins Milly and Molly were all knocked out, which meant racing to the finish were Felicity Bat, Peggy, and Tiga. Luckily, Peggy knocked Felicity Bat out of the competition! Much to everyone's surprise.

Tiga and Peggy then had to decide who was going to win, because there can be only one ruling witch. They each wanted the other to win, but Tiga knew Peggy had to win; it was her dream, and she had lots of great ideas to make Sinkville better.

So Peggy became Top Witch, and back up the pipes Tiga went, to confront the evil Miss Heks, who, she had found out, HAD BEEN THE ONE TO PUT TIGA FORWARD FOR WITCH WARS!

Miss Heks had been one of the witches who left Sinkville during the Big Exit, when a bunch of evil witches left for a life above the pipes and took their

houses and shops and all the color in Sinkville with them. Greedy.

Tiga was pretty sure she'd be stuck with horrible Miss Heks forever, but then Peggy, Fran, Fluffanora, and her mom, Mrs. Brew, came up the sink pipes, and Mrs. Brew said she would adopt Tiga and take her back down to Ritzy City, where she belonged!

Miss Heks was like, "SURE! Take her!" or something like that. She probably said it in a much more evil way.

Tiga put her pet slug in her pocket and back down they went to Ritzy City!

When they arrived, everyone was talking about how the witch with the cart of disgusting hats had been very wrong. When predicting the winner of Witch Wars, she had said, "An elegant witch will rule this land, and that bossy one will lend a hand. Witch sisters, maybe, but not the same. One is dear, the other? A PAIN. And, much like the tales of times gone by, they will find a sweet apple and … My oh my, is that the time? I'd better go."

3

Everyone thought, because Peggy wasn't really *elegant* as such, that the witch had gotten it wrong—and there was no bossy witch helping Peggy, and the apple bit made no sense. But when we left them, the witch with the disgusting hats was smiling. Why? Well, because she knew everything, and she knew exactly what was going to happen next.

And what she knew was going to happen, happens to be happening RIGHT NOW.

The Cauldron Islands

"I HATE it here!" Fluffanora roared, kicking her foot and sending an extremely sparkly shoe sailing across the room.

"Frogs," Tiga groaned as it hit her square in the face.

They had been on the Cauldron Islands for two whole weeks and Fluffanora had been flinging shoes since they'd arrived.

The Cauldron Islands were where the Brews spent their summers. It had once been home to all the cauldron factories, but since witches had stopped using cauldrons, except perhaps for storing shoes or hitting burglars with, the factories had closed down. Mrs. Brew had bought the largest cauldron factory, Crinkle Cauldrons—it once had the best cauldrons and you could tell them apart

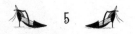

from other cauldrons because they had crinkly looking handles. A lot of witches had complained that the crinkle in the cauldron made it impossible to hold, and so many spilled their potions and burned their feet, but Tina Gloop, the owner of Crinkle Cauldrons, said they obviously just had shaky hands.

When Crinkle Cauldrons closed down, Mrs. Brew converted the factory into a huge summer house. A bunch of other Ritzy City witches read about it in *Toad* magazine and copied her, and the neighboring islands were also revamped. The murky waters were cleaned up and Bubble Beach, owned by Berta Bubble, was soon peppered with vacation houses and fun little clubs, including the two most popular ones: the Hubble Hut, popular with the Brews and other witches from Ritzy City, and the Toil & Trouble Tavern, which was frequented by evil witches and the Pearl Peak families.

Tiga and Fluffanora had peeked into the Toil & Trouble Tavern on the first day they arrived and spotted a bunch of witches twirling around in the middle of the room to a really evil song called "I Want to Curse Your

Loved Ones," by the Silver Rats, a weird band Fluffanora described as "complete slime." Apparently they were Aggie Hoof's absolute favorite band. Fluffanora had shown Tiga a picture—there were three of them, all dressed in tutus with chunky black boots, and they had little rat ears poking out the tops of their hats, and their faces were painted silver.

The Hubble Hut was much better, and it served Clutterbucks drinks.

"Tiga, is your head all right?" Mrs. Brew cried as she raced over to her.

"I've accidentally hit her with seven shoes in the last two days," Fluffanora began.

"*Nine*," Tiga said through gritted teeth.

Fluffanora shrugged. "She's *fine*. She has a strong head."

"Fluffanora," Mrs. Brew snapped, "you have been behaving terribly."

"Well then, let me go back to Ritzy!" Fluffanora shouted back.

It was well known throughout Sinkville that

Fluffanora was not a fan of the Cauldron Islands. Everyone knew this because *Toad* magazine had once featured an article called "Fluffanora Is Not a Fan of the Cauldron Islands." It had described Fluffanora's various attempts over the years to escape vacations there. There was the time she had ten thousand cats delivered to Bubble Beach and ran around screaming, "OH NO, THE PLAGUE OF CATS! RUN, SAVE YOURSELVES!" Or the time she paid the old witch with the cart of disgusting hats to walk up and down the beach shouting, "GENUINE HATS WHAT GOT STUCK IN THE PIPES! GENUINE HATS WHAT GOT STUCK IN THE PIPES!" to annoy everyone. Fluffanora had even attempted to make cauldrons cool again, hoping that if cauldrons were in demand, they would need the Cauldron Islands' factories back.

None of her attempts worked. Especially not that cat one. Most witches would welcome a plague of cats. They can't get enough of them.

Unlike Fluffanora, Tiga *loved* the Cauldron Islands. There was so much fun stuff to do—like wartling

9

(almost the same as snorkeling, only instead of a snorkel and mask, you use magic giant warts to cover your whole face, so you can breathe underwater). Tiga spent hours exploring the cool caves and underwater walkways below Bubble Beach. The weird thing was, there wasn't a single fish, just lots of frogs dressed in different outfits—there was one in a stripy dress and one wearing a small box hat. She did spot one frog *dressed* as a fish, sitting on a rock, sipping out of a shell cup next to a frog dressed as a mermaid.

Mrs. Brew had explained to Tiga that you would never find a fish near the Cauldron Islands. They had decided to swim away to the north of Sinkville, around the Coves area, because they found the frogs insufferable.

"*PLEASE*, can we go home? I want to go to Clutterbucks," Fluffanora begged.

Mrs. Brew shook her head. "You can drink Clutterbucks at the Hubble Hut. You need a better reason than that to go back."

Little did the three of them know, sitting in the cauldron-shaped mailbox outside was a letter containing a very, *very* good reason to go back . . .

Fran in a Trailer

Fran was the first one to notice Peggy was missing.

The fairy had been stopping by Linden House to "help" (boss around) Peggy every day since she'd become Top Witch, suggesting changes like creating a huge statue of Fran, painting a gigantic mural on the front of Linden House (of Fran), and changing the name of the city to FRAN. However, there were two days when she hadn't visited Peggy—and it was during that time that Peggy had VANISHED.

It had been a particularly windy couple of days in Sinkville, and Fran's trailer, which hung precariously from a tree in Brollywood, had proved impossible to get out of—every time she pushed the door open, the wind blew it shut again.

She had tried 9,846 times to get out.

She had even tried squeezing out of the tiny window, but her big beehive of hair wouldn't fit.

"HELP! I'M STUCK IN MY TRAILER, MY ADORING FANS! GET ME OUT!" she cried, but no one heard. Apart from perhaps Julie, who flew past a few times.

"Is that you, Julie Jumbo Wings?! JULIE JUMBO WINGS?!"

Julie had simply held her head high and carried on flying.

According to her, she heard nothing.

When the wind eventually died down, Fran emerged from the trailer, her hair all lopsided and her dress curled up in the corners like a disgruntled flower. She blew away the piece of hair dangling in her face and shot off toward Linden House.

She zoomed high over the Docks, which Peggy had gotten straight to work on when she had been crowned Top Witch. The Docks, where Peggy came from, had been a bit grubby, but she soon fixed up lots of the houses—repairing wobbly floors and sewing holey curtains. And for the witches whose houses were beyond repair, Peggy had convinced Mrs. Brew to donate beautiful shoes, and then she had done the shoe spell, which many witches all over Sinkville had watched her do during Witch Wars. ("Little laces and heels in a heap, make me a better place to sleep.")

As well as making some very nice shoe-shaped houses, Peggy had sat outside Linden House on the first day of her reign and asked witches to tell her what they needed help with and what they would like to see changed. She had helped lots of witches. Old Hilda Trip had asked for new legs because hers were very old and hurt when she walked too far. Peggy couldn't really do anything about that, but she did make a very excellent flying armchair for Old Hilda. And a young witch named Alice Spoon said she'd really love to be a baker, but she didn't know where to start, so Peggy got her an apprenticeship at Cakes, Pies, and That's About It Really, the baker's. Fran had asked for a National Fran Day. Peggy said she would think about it.

"Peggy!" Fran cried as she flew toward the window Peggy always left open for her, "I have been in the greatest peril! I was stuck in my trailer for two days! With no access to my hairdresser!"

She sped up, "Pegg—"

THUD!

The window was closed!

Squeak

Squeak

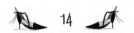

14

Squeeeeak

... went Fran as she slid all the way down to the pavement, where she finally plopped into a little heap.

She barely had time to be furious about the fact that Peggy had closed the window when the door to Linden House flew open.

Fran raised a finger, ready to give Peggy a good telling-off. But all she did was gasp.

There, standing proudly in all her evil glory, was none other than Felicity Bat. And next to her was her smug sidekick, Aggie Hoof.

3

A Far-from-Fabulous Note

"What does it say?" Fluffanora asked, eagerly peering over Tiga's shoulder at the note she had pulled from the cauldron-shaped mailbox.

Tiga shook her head in disbelief and read it out loud.

> *Dearest Tiga,*
>
> *My hair is A MESS, my wing is slightly crushed, and there is also a third thing that is ALMOST as terrible as those things that I must tell you.*

"She's run out of glittery dust, hasn't she?" Fluffanora said, rolling her eyes.

Tiga carried on.

 16

I can't find Peggy. Not only can I not find her, but Felicity Bat has taken over Linden House! She and Aggie Hoof said Peggy left and put them in charge. Apparently she left them a note saying she was "going away with the fairies."

I immediately knew this was ridiculous non-sense. Why? Because the fairies are all far too busy to go away anywhere. Most of them are working on Crispy's new horror film, TOE PINCHERS, apart from Donna, who is just being lazy. And there is Julie Jumbo Wings . . . but Peggy wouldn't go anywhere with her. And anyway, Julie definitely flew past my trailer yesterday and ignored my cries for help.

I'm not sure what to do.

COME BACK TO RITZY CITY.

(Please also find enclosed a signed photo of my face.)

Thank you.

Your Very Fabulous Fairy,

Fran

"We must go back to Ritzy City right now!" Tiga cried.

Fluffanora practically exploded with excitement. "YES!"

She raced upstairs to pack.

"Wait!" Mrs. Brew said, waving a finger and gluing Fluffanora to the spot.

"Unstick me!" she shouted, trying to lift her feet off the ground.

Mrs. Brew sighed and studied the letter carefully.

"It sounds like Peggy might be in trouble . . . ," Tiga muttered.

"Okay," Mrs. Brew said reluctantly. "But I don't want you traveling by road. If Felicity Bat is up to something, she will expect you to arrive in my car. I can't imagine she will be pleased to see you. You should take the cauldron."

She flicked a finger and Fluffanora tumbled back down the stairs.

Tiga raised an eyebrow. It was something Tiga had been doing almost daily since arriving in Ritzy City. Most of the time she didn't have a frogs what was going on.

"I'll send these two back to the house by road,"

Mrs. Brew said, pointing at Tiga's slug and Fluffanora's cat, Mrs. Pumpkin. "Mrs. Pumpkin would only panic in the cauldron."

Mrs. Pumpkin hissed.

"FREEDOM!" Fluffanora cried.

She grabbed Tiga's arm and dragged her along the crinkled corridor and out onto the crinkled patio overlooking the not-at-all-crinkled sea. Tied up in the corner was a large cauldron with a crinkled handle.

A silky white sail was sticking out of the top.

"Is that a boat?" Tiga asked.

"No, it's a cauldron," said Fluffanora.

Meanwhile, at Linden House...

"I'm not sure how long we're going to get away with this, Fel-Fel," Aggie Hoof said as she swept some papers and an old doll off the sofa, plonked herself down, and flicked through the latest copy of *Toad*. "Did you know, Fel-Fel, that you can never have too many pairs of shoes? That's what it says right here. It doesn't matter that you only have two feet, you know. You can just keep ... on ... buying ... shoes. Fashion never fails to amaze me."

Felicity Bat didn't bother to answer. She was busy having her portrait painted by Lady Frank, who painted all the official Top Witch portraits. It was only a few weeks since she'd painted one of Peggy, who had tried to make her hair nice for it but had somehow managed to rearrange the hair completely so it was on her chin. It looked very much like she had a gigantic, fuzzy beard.

Felicity Bat straightened her hat. "Make sure I look terrifying, Lady Frank."

Lady Frank nodded.

"What if Tiga tries to find Peggy?" Aggie Hoof asked. "Fran will definitely tell her that Peggy's missing."

Felicity Bat cackled. "She won't find her. Anyway, the precious Brew family is still on vacation in the

Cauldron Islands, and I have spies on the road. If Tiga comes back, I'll know about it."

"What about Fluffanora?" Aggie Hoof asked.

Felicity Bat shrugged.

"She really likes Peggy too," Aggie Hoof went on. "And she really likes fashion, which is annoying because that's my thing. And I do it better, don't I?"

"Uh-huh," Felicity Bat mumbled as Lady Frank flicked her finger and sploshed more paint on the canvas.

"What if they come here and I accidentally tell them that Peggy is hidden in—"

"QUIET!" Felicity Bat shouted. Aggie Hoof was so irritating and she didn't need her anymore, but Felicity couldn't get rid of her now. She knew too much . . .

"I know," Felicity Bat said, snaking over to Aggie Hoof and putting an arm around her. "Because you love fashion so much, why don't *you* become the editor of *Toad* magazine. That'll show Fluffanora."

"But how?" Aggie Hoof asked, her eyes as wide as cauldrons.

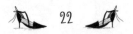

"Well, we can just make the current editor *disappear*. I am in charge of this place, after all. Slowly and quietly we are going to get rid of every good witch in Ritzy City."

"You can make Darcy Dream disappear and make me the editor of *Toad*, Fel-Fel?"

Felicity Bat nodded.

With that, Aggie Hoof leapt in the air and spun around the room, knocking over almost everything that could be knocked over, including Felicity Bat and the painting Lady Frank had almost finished.

"On one condition," Felicity Bat said, pulling herself upright again.

"Yes, Fel-Fel?"

She leaned into Aggie Hoof and whispered in her ear, "You are not allowed to tell anyone what I did to Peggy."

"DEEEEEEAAAAAAAL!" Aggie Hoof said as she spun around some more.

They both cackled, and Peggy, from the really squashed place where she was trapped, could hear it all.

5

Cauldrons Ahoy!

Tiga mumbled a few words, waved her hand, and grinned as her hair twisted itself up into a neat bun. Fluffanora flicked her finger, and a stripy dress, a long white coat, some sunglasses, and an extra-large floppy hat came sailing down from the bedroom and flew into her arms.

"It's my sailing outfit," she said defensively as Tiga smiled.

They climbed inside the cauldron, which was surprisingly roomy. There was a little ledge around the bottom with cushions to sit on, and above it sat a platform with a big steering wheel. Fluffanora stood next to it, her hat flapping about in the wind.

"Good luck, girls!" Mrs. Brew called to them from

24

the balcony. "And remember, Tiga, if you find yourself in trouble, send me the signal."

Tiga had learned the secret signal in the Brew household. It was used if anyone in the family was in trouble. The signal was a small fat spider named Sid whom you could call on to land on the head of the person you needed to come and rescue you. He would jump up and down on the person's head screaming "TROUBLE! TROUBLE TROOOOUBLE!" until she came and saved you.

Fluffanora wasn't allowed to use Sid anymore, because she tended to use him for things like "I'M BORED" and "Can you come and pick me up from Clutterbucks?" Neither of which, Mrs. Brew had pointed out, was an emergency.

"Which way do we go?" Tiga asked, waving a Sinkville map she'd spotted in the bottom of the cauldron.

Fluffanora flicked her finger, and a slim little frog wearing a skirt shot out of the water into her hand. She looked at it and said: "Scream and sing and

sometimes squeak. I give you, quiet thing, the power to SPEAK!"

She held it up to her eye like a telescope. "What can you see?" she asked.

"Your eyeball on one side, and a clear route to Ritzy City. The sea is calm," said the frog.

"DID THAT FROG JUST TALK?" Tiga spluttered.

"Also," said the frog, "Mrs. Brew is wearing a very large and fussy hat, which I think might be too much."

"It *is* too much," Fluffanora said.

The frog smacked its lips.

"GO! GO! GO! GO! GOOOOOOO!" Fluffanora shouted. "Tiga, hold on."

Tiga grabbed the wheel, and the cauldron soared off around the edge of Bubble Beach and out into the silky gray expanse of sea.

Fluffanora tapped the map in Tiga's hand. "You guide me. I say we park in the Docks and walk to Ritzy from there. We don't want to dock in Ritzy."

Tiga studied the map. They'd have to sail past Ritzy City to get to the Docks . . .

"DANGER AHEAD!" the frog bellowed.

6

Twins and Squid

As the cauldron boat swirled around in the choppy water, Tiga leaned as far over the edge as she could and scanned the sea.

"I can't see any danger!" she shouted back to Fluffanora.

"Me neither!" Fluffanora had accidentally dropped the slippery little frog back in the water before it had explained exactly what the danger was, and now she couldn't find it. She flicked her finger and started grabbing the frogs that popped out of the water—one in a tie, one wearing some sunglasses, another wearing a wig. "No, wasn't you!" she kept shouting.

Tiga began climbing up the pole that held the silky

sail. She got all the way to the top before she saw what was coming.

In the distance she could just make out two figures speeding toward the cauldron boat. She recognized the ballooning skirts and the bristly little tufts of hair sticking out of their hats right away.

"Milly and Molly!" Tiga shouted.

"What?" Fluffanora said, flinging a frog in some spotted pants back into the water. "They are hardly a *danger*."

Tiga frantically pointed in their direction.

"Ah," said Fluffanora when she saw the gigantic black square thing with teeth they were riding on. "That's a Cauldron Eater 5000."

"A WHAT?" Tiga cried.

Fluffanora rolled up her sleeves. "The Cauldron Eater 5000s were created when the cauldron factories were shut down. Many of the cauldrons that went to waste were just dumped in the water, which of course made a mess of the sea. The Cauldron Eater 5000s were designed to swim around and eat the cauldrons, to clean

the place up. But then it became fashionable to create boats made out of old cauldrons . . . and, well, we didn't ever find all of the Cauldron Eater 5000s—some of them went rogue."

Milly and Molly were getting closer now. Tiga could hear their cackles loud and clear.

"So that thing they are riding will *eat* us?"

Fluffanora nodded.

Tiga threw her arms in the air. "How are we going to stop it?!"

"We can't," said Fluffanora.

"We can't?" asked Tiga.

"We can't," said Fluffanora. "Unless I can think of something very quickly."

Tiga prodded her arm. "THINK OF SOMETHING QUICKLY!"

Fluffanora stared as they floated closer and closer. "Ah! If we huddle down in the bottom of the cauldron, we might make it."

"*MIGHT?!*" Tiga howled.

Fluffanora shrugged.

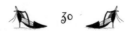

"SIIIIIIIIIID!" Tiga squealed. "SIIIIIIIIIID! Sid the warning spider will let Mrs. Brew know we're in danger and then she can help!"

There was a loud bang and a cloud of smoke appeared in front of Tiga, with something written in spindly, spider-like letters:

SID IS CURRENTLY ON VACATION AND WILL RESPOND TO THIS EMERGENCY WHEN HE GETS BACK—IN TWO WEEKS' TIME.

Tiga gawped at the message.

Fluffanora stepped forward and tapped Tiga's jaw closed. "Not even Sid can help you now. Not that Sid can normally help anyway . . ."

Milly and Molly waved sinister little waves. They were only moments away.

Fluffanora held her breath. Tiga squeezed her eyes shut. A massive horn honked.

HOOOONK. HOOOONK. HONK. HONK.

A huge shadow descended. Slowly, they both looked

up. So did Milly and Molly and their Cauldron Eater 5000.

Just above them hovered a familiar witch with two feather dusters strapped to her feet.

"LIZZIE BEAST!" Tiga and Fluffanora shouted as Lizzie Beast made another honking noise.

"*HONK!*"

She reached down and grabbed them by their collars, yanking them up high into the air.

Milly and Molly growled as the three of them sped off into the distance. The Cauldron Eater 5000's eyes swiveled around and stared up intently at Milly and Molly, who weren't cauldrons but *might* be just as tasty.

"*Eeep!*" Molly said. She nodded her head and just like that, she and her sister vanished.

TOAD
MAGAZINE

Witches of Sinkville, HOLD ON TO YOUR INFERIOR WARDROBES! It's me, Aggie Hoof, your new *Toad* editor.

Darcy Dream has decided she doesn't want to be the editor of *Toad* magazine anymore and is playing hide-and-seek on her own instead.

And you shouldn't look for her because it would be really nice for her if she won the game of hide-and-seek that she's playing on her own.

In honor of this being the first ever issue of *Toad* magazine edited by me, I have made the whole thing about ME. You are going to be totally inspired...

THE STORY OF MY FIRST PAIR OF SHOES

These days I have so many pairs of shoes, but a long time ago I had only one pair of

shoes. I wasn't even one year old and MY feet were finally big enough for small shoes. My mom took me to Crow Toes in Pearl Peak to get my first pair. My bestest friend, Felicity Bat, came too, but she cried the whole time because she was scared of the crow on the sign. It's not a scary crow at all, see:

Then I got some shoes—stripy with lots of bows on them—and took a nap.

THE END.

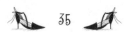

7

A Lift from Lizzie

Meanwhile, high up above Sinkville on the shoulders of Lizzie Beast . . .

"I bet Felicity Bat ordered Milly and Molly to police the seas on that cauldron eater thing. That's totally something she would do . . . ," Tiga mumbled to herself, hanging awkwardly from Lizzie Beast's neck. Fluffanora was higher up, on Tiga's shoulders. The whole thing would have been dangerous on land, but when zooming through the air on some feather dusters, it was positively DEADLY.

"Don't slip," Lizzie Beast said as Tiga flopped forward and nearly somersaulted right off her.

"Did you hear about Peggy?" Tiga asked.

Lizzie Beast nodded furiously as Tiga tried to hold

on to her head. "Terrible. And it's obviously Felicity Bat's fault. Peggy's mom was on *Brollywood News* just about an hour ago, right before I picked you up, and she said, 'Peggy *has* gone away with the fairies. Peggy *has* gone away with the fairies.' Everyone believed it, but her eyes were funny. They were big and black, and I think someone had put a spell on her."

Tiga shook her head. "It must have been Felicity Bat and Aggie Hoof. Those PAINS."

"What have you been up to, Lizzie Beast?" Fluffanora asked. "What were you doing here?"

"I've been helping my mom in Brollywood. She's working on the new fairy film *Toe Pinchers*. She sent me to the Cauldron Islands to see if we could find another fairy—they need one more because Bow the fairy keeps not showing up."

"No-show Bow," Tiga said.

"*Who?*" Fluffanora asked.

"She was Peggy's fairy in Witch Wars, but she didn't show up," Tiga said.

"Ah!" said Fluffanora. "No-show Bow!"

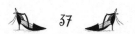

37

Lizzie Beast took a sharp left and wobbled around dangerously on the feather dusters.

"Is the film any good?" Fluffanora asked. "Balance, Tiga!"

Lizzie Beast shrugged and almost sent them both flying. "It's very funny, you know, watching the fairies scuttling about trying to be scary. Crispy has to say, 'He he he, I'm going to slightly puncture the tip of your toe with my tiny little fang!' It's meant to be a horror film, but, well, it's not."

Tiga laughed as they soared lower. She could make out the tall buildings of Ritzy City poking through the clouds up ahead.

"Where do you want me to drop you off?" Lizzie Beast asked as they tore through the sky, and the bustling city and all its weird witches came into focus.

"Take us to my house, 99 Ritzy City Avenue," Fluffanora shouted down to her. "But take the back route. We don't want to soar up the avenue right past Linden House!"

"That would be SILLY!" Lizzie Beast said with a chuckle.

Unfortunately, when Lizzie Beast chuckles, her shoulders tend to shake dramatically and so before Tiga knew what was happening, she felt herself flying off Lizzie Beast and tumbling fast toward the ground.

"Oh frogmuppets," she heard Fluffanora grumble as she too somersaulted down and down.

Lizzie Beast shot after them, but didn't see the roof to her left, banged into it, and went swirling off in the other direction.

"Sooooorrrrrryyyyyyyyyyyy," she said before crashing through the roof of Cakes, Pies, and That's About It Really.

Tiga was headed for a different roof entirely.

BANG!

She peeled her face off the soft canvas roofing of the stall she'd just fallen on. It was the exact same stall she'd fallen on when she first landed in Ritzy City.

"Hello, I'm Mavis, would you like some ja— Oh it's just you, Tiga," said Mavis, putting the jar of jam back on the shelf.

"Sorry about the damage," Tiga said with a guilty

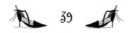

grin as she looked around for Fluffanora. She was usually easy to spot in a crowd—she was always the one in an elaborate hat or a ridiculous skirt. Sometimes both.

Tiga looked up and down the street.

"Fluffanora?" she whispered. "Um . . . Fluffanora?"

"Is *that* her?" Mavis asked, pointing at what seemed to be a witch being attacked by at least seventy cats. "The witch who normally looks after that stall—Norris is her name—is missing. Very strange. She is always there every morning, standing right there. But she wasn't there yesterday or today. No one can find her . . ."

"I fell on the Jam and Cats stall, Tiga!" Fluffanora cried as a cat attached itself to her face.

"That's unlucky," said Mavis. "All the other stalls just sell jam."

Tiga glanced around nervously at all the witches staring at them. So much for sneaking into Ritzy City without being noticed.

Every witch and her cat knew they were back in town. And so did two complete *pains*.

"Well, well, well," said Felicity Bat, gliding down the street. "You survived the wild seas of Sinkville."

Tiga stood taller. "I *knew* it was you who sent Milly and Molly after us!"

"Is that Fluffanora?" Aggie Hoof asked. "Wait, are we wearing cats now? Is that a thing? WHY DID NO ONE TELL ME?!"

The Sort-of Great Escape

"What have you done with Peggy?" Tiga said, grabbing Felicity Bat's arm.

Felicity Bat just cackled.

Tiga asked again.

"*Nothing*," Felicity Bat said with a smirk. "She left completely by herself."

"And we're meant to believe she put *you* in charge?" Fluffanora said as she pulled huge clumps of cat hair off her hat.

"That is what we want you to believe, yes," said Aggie Hoof.

Felicity Bat elbowed her.

"Because it's definitely not a lie," Aggie Hoof added.

Felicity Bat rolled her eyes.

"Where is the evidence that she put you in charge?" Tiga demanded.

Aggie Hoof flung a piece of paper in her face.

Fluffanora peered over Tiga's shoulder.

"Yeah," said Fluffanora. "You've signed it with *your* name and then crossed it out."

I am going away with the fairies. Please ensure
Felicity Bat takes care of everything until I return.
  Sincerely,
  ~~Aggie Hoof~~ *Peggy*

"She obviously got confused," Aggie Hoof mumbled with a sideways glance at Felicity Bat.

"Look," said Felicity Bat, getting impatient. "I am in charge here, and you are both coming with me. RIGHT. NOW."

"Right now," Aggie Hoof added unnecessarily.

"No, we're not," Tiga said.

"*Yes*, we *are*," Fluffanora said with a wink.

". . . Are we?" Tiga asked.

 43

Fluffanora nodded insistently.

"Okay . . . ," Tiga said. She had no idea what was going on.

"This way," Aggie Hoof said, pointing down Ritzy Avenue.

Felicity Bat flew faster. "Hurry up," she snapped.

Fluffanora smiled. "Oh, look over there! Mom's new collection of dresses. People say this season's collection is her best yet. They say the dresses are the best Sinkville has EVER SEEN."

Of course that sent Aggie Hoof pelting toward the Brew's shop window. She smooshed her face up against it and said, "Ooooh."

Felicity Bat had soared on ahead.

"Quick," Tiga hissed at Fluffanora. "Let's escape!"

"I'd already thought of that," said Fluffanora as she grabbed Tiga's arm and ducked down a side alley. They reached a familiar little door. Fluffanora knocked on it seven times, drummed her fingers once, and knocked once more.

9

Clutterbucks!

Clutterbucks was packed to bursting with witches floating about on chairs and drinking bubbly drinks.

"Well, of course you can hide out in here, dears," said Mrs. Clutterbuck, plonking a huge cake down in front of them. "That's the last cake, though. Our cake chef has vanished. I can't find her anywhere. Weird things have been happening in Ritzy City lately. Witches, just vanishing! Some people, sensible people, think it's that Felicity Bat doing it, but who knows how! Others keep saying, 'Well, if Peggy put her in charge she must be good, because Peggy wouldn't do something to put any of us in danger.' They don't see what's happening!"

"We're going to find Peggy, Mrs. Clutterbuck," Tiga

said confidently. "We're going to fix everything, aren't we, Fluffanora?"

Fluffanora was face deep in cake and unavailable to answer.

"They'll find us eventually if we stay here, though," Tiga said, staring at Fluffanora. "If only we hadn't fallen off Lizzie Beast . . ."

"Well, it's done now, and we have a bit of time at least," Fluffanora said as she came up for air.

There was a loud knock at the door.

Not the seven secret knocks that you're meant to do. Just two loud knocks.

Mrs. Clutterbuck scuttled over and opened the little hatch in the door.

"It's them!" she hissed, slamming the hatch shut again. "I'll have to let them in. Felicity Bat is technically the new ruler of Sinkville . . ."

Bang, bang, bang. "Let us in," Felicity Bat said.

"Just a minute!" Mrs. Clutterbuck called sweetly. A bead of sweat dribbled down her nose and plopped into a We-Hate-Celia-Crayfish cocktail.

"We could always hide in the world above the pipes! Sneak out the back and up a pipe!" Tiga cried. "They would never look there."

"I think it's pretty safe to say Felicity Bat will be guarding the pipes," Mrs. Clutterbuck rambled nervously. "She knows you know that world well, Tiga. She'd expect you to hide back up there."

"Well, we can't let them find us," Tiga said. "They'd only do something to get us out of the way. Probably whatever they've done to Peggy!"

Boom, boom, boom!

The knocks were getting louder now.

"Oh, boom, boom, BOOM," Fluffanora said, rolling her eyes. "She's a complete pain!"

Tiga leapt to her feet.

"I know what to do!" she cried. "The BOOM!"

She grabbed the Clutterbucks menu and waved it in Fluffanora's face.

CLUTTERBUCKS
Makers of the best bubbly drinks since
winks were invented

Ritzy Original—5 sinkels
The Witching Whirl—8 sinkels
Flat-Hat Fizz—6 sinkels
The We-Hate-Celia-Crayfish Cocktail—6 sinkels
Witch Wars Mix—5 sinkels
The Big-Exit Bubble Mix—5 sinkels
Brilliant Big Sue Supreme—8 sinkels
The Peggy Pigwiggle Punch—8 sinkels
BOOM*—9,000 sinkels

*WARNING: This drink transports you back in
time for ten minutes to Ritzy City a hundred years
ago. (Two hundred years ago if you drink it
through your nose.)

"What? Go back in time?" Fluffanora said.

BOOM, BOOM, BOOM. "If you don't let us in, we will huff and we will puff and we will then kick the door until we have knocked it down!" Felicity Bat said.

"I'm not kicking the door. Look at *my shoes*," they heard Aggie Hoof say.

Mrs. Clutterbuck shakily poured out some BOOM drink.

Fluffanora pulled 18,000 sinkels out of her pocket.

Thank *frogs* they only needed to go back a hundred years, so Tiga didn't have to drink the thing through her nose.

"Good luck, dears," Mrs. Clutterbuck said as they downed the drinks. Mrs. Clutterbuck's voice instantly warped and became all funny—kind of like someone with a really squeaky voice speaking underwater.

Within seconds, it felt like they had turned to jelly and someone was gently rolling them down a hill.

The knocking faded into the distance, and they could just about make out Mrs. Clutterbuck saying, "They aren't here, Felicity Bat . . ."

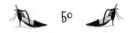 50

BOOM!

Pretty soon, there was nothing but a bright white light and silence. Then Fluffanora said, from somewhere Tiga couldn't see, "Is *this* what a hundred years ago looked like? It's BORING."

BOOM!

The pair of them were all of a sudden magically smack-dab back in Clutterbucks, but not the Clutterbucks they knew. Not the Clutterbucks they had just left.

There was no Felicity Bat and the place was awash with bright colors! Not the usual black, white, and gray. And everyone was wearing huge dresses with big ruffles on the bottoms and much smaller hats.

Tiga glanced around the room in amazement. Instead of the fancy Clutterbucks drinks machines, there were cauldrons bubbling everywhere, and Mrs. Clutterbuck looked about twelve.

"Welcome to the past, dears!" she cried. "Future me hasn't sent anyone back on the BOOM in a very long time. I was worried something terrible had happened in the future! Like a spell had gotten out of hand and everyone had accidentally been turned into jam. Jam that was then eaten by some birds."

"That's quite a specific worry," Fluffanora said.

Mrs. Clutterbuck spooned some liquid from the cauldron into two thin glasses. "When you want to go back, you drink these. Remember to drink it before the time is up, or you will be stuck in the past FOREVER."

Two other women popped up from behind the counter. They looked identical to Mrs. Clutterbuck.

"Hello, I'm Mrs. Clutterbuck," one of them said.

"And so am I," said the other.

Tiga stared at them blankly. "*Three* Mrs. Clutterbucks?"

"Oh yes," said the first Mrs. Clutterbuck. "We three sisters run this place."

"Clutterbucks was started by the three of them," Fluffanora whispered. "Two of them vanished during the Big Exit—went above the pipes with the evil witches."

Tiga eyed the other two suspiciously as they grinned and blinked at her.

They didn't *look* very evil . . .

Tiga turned around slowly and took everything in. All the floating tables and chairs in Clutterbucks were the same, and the cakes. Lots of witches looked down at her from their floating chairs and waved. In a little cove in the wall a cluster of fairies was acting out some sort of play. One witch was holding up a crooked wand and flicking it in their direction.

"Is she controlling them like puppets?" Tiga asked.

The witch flicked her wand again and sent a fairy soaring up and crashing back down. "Now dance!" she cried as the other witches burst into a chorus of cackles and clapped.

Fluffanora nodded. "Fairies were just things to play with in the olden days. They didn't have any rights. They were kept like pets. And witches didn't have TVs they could watch on the backs of spoons, so they would do live shows instead."

One of the fairies looked suspiciously like a very young Fran.

"*I* think the play would be *much* better if you changed my line to—"

"BE QUIET, FAIRY!" the witch shouted.

"That's Fran!" Tiga cried.

The fairy looked up in amazement. "A fan?" she mouthed, clutching her heart.

Tiga waved.

"Some things never change," Fluffanora said with a smile.

"Why don't witches use wands anymore?" Tiga asked. "I haven't seen any around Ritzy City."

Fluffanora ran her finger along the edge of a cake and swirled the icing into a neat clump. "Wands look like twigs, Tiga. They are silly."

"Witches stopped using wands because they looked *silly*?"

"Nah, that's just my opinion," Fluffanora explained. "No, actually, wands were only used by witches for a brief spell of time, only for two hundred years or so. Traditionally witches used their fingers or made potions in cauldrons or spoke spells out loud. Then a very brash witch called Hilda Yoohoo!—that exclamation mark is part of her name—created wands and made them fashionable, said it was a great way for witches to enhance their spells. Apparently she got the idea when she went above the pipes and saw non-witches using these things called chopsticks to eat their food. Originally, when wands were first introduced, witches actually used *two* wands, like chopsticks, to cast spells. But that looked nuts, so they stopped."

"I can imagine," said Tiga with a smile.

"After a while, the fashion for wands faded and witches just started using their fingers again, sometimes decorating them instead. Like this." Fluffanora pulled a long piece of silver chain out of her pocket—it was covered in little silver stars. She wrapped it around her finger from top to bottom. "A witch doesn't *need* a wand, you see. All the magic ultimately comes from the finger."

"OUCH!" a witch yelled from the corner of the room. She was holding a hand over her eye.

"Also, *a lot* of witches kept accidentally poking other witches in the eye."

Tiga giggled as the witch covering her eye threw a drink at her friend and shouted, "Why did you have to get the massive FORTY-SEVEN-INCH ONE, SUE?!"

"Anyway, that's enough on the history of the wand. We're running out of time, Tiga—what should our plan be?" Fluffanora asked. "Do we just wait here until the time is up?"

"That's all we can do, isn't it?"

"I suppose so . . ." Fluffanora said as a woman they both recognized glided past. She was wearing a floaty yellow dress covered in black and orange swirls. Her hat, like everyone else's, was small—but it had a

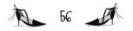

massive, fluffy pom-pom sitting on top of it. It looked, well, ridiculously fabulous.

"EDDY EGGBY!" they roared.

Eddy Eggby was a famous fashion explorer (whatever that is) from the past whom Tiga had once learned about from the ancient Coves witches. Tiga had given Eddy Eggby's fashion notes to Fluffanora as a present and it was fair to say that Fluffanora had since become OBSESSED with her. The strange thing was, no one knew what had happened to Eddy Eggby. About a hundred years ago she had just disappeared . . .

"Fluffanora," Tiga said. "This is a hundred years ago, around the time Eddy Eggby went missing!"

Eddy Eggby was eagerly swanning toward them, clearly intrigued by these two strangers who knew who she was and were clad in such strange clothes.

"Eddy Eggby, Fashion Explorer," she said confidently, shaking Fluffanora's hand.

Fluffanora nearly fell off her seat.

"We're from the future," Tiga said, without thinking for a second how ridiculous that sounded.

57

But Eddy Eggby wasn't surprised at all. "Ah, that explains the clothes. I thought I'd missed a new fashion. You've been on the BOOM."

"Oh, Eddy Eggby," Fluffanora butted in. "I think something is going to happen to y—"

"WHOOPS!" cried Mrs. Clutterbuck as she *accidentally* tipped an entire cauldron of juice over Fluffanora before she could finish her warning.

"You can't mess with the past," she whispered.

Tiga nodded and took a different approach. "Where are you off to now, Eddy Eggby?"

"Oh, above the pipes, of course! I need to stop off and see Cornelia Crayfish first, one of our old ruling witches. Her darling daughter, Celia, just turned one today. I'm going to give her this Clutterbucks drinks machine as a birthday gift—it's a prototype, they haven't started using them yet! Very special. It was wonderful to meet you both. Perhaps we will catch up and have a Clutterbucks in the future when I am much, much older!"

"Perhaps . . . ," mumbled Fluffanora as she flicked

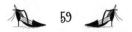

her finger and tried to magic a hair dryer over her juice-soaked head. Of course, they didn't exist in the olden days, so a huge old rag fell on her instead.

And off Eddy Eggby went.

Fluffanora ripped the rag off her head and turned to Tiga with her mouth hanging open. "Oh. My. FROGS."

"What?" Tiga asked. But she knew what Fluffanora was getting at. Celia Crayfish, the baby Eddy Eggby just mentioned, was Felicity Bat's grandmother. When she grew up she had become a ruling witch, the worst of the lot, most people said, apart from her fans.

Fluffanora raised a finger in the air. "I think Celia Crayfish did something terrible to Eddy Eggby."

"You think a *one-year-old* did something terrible to Eddy Eggby?" Tiga asked.

Fluffanora nodded. "*YES*. I think we've landed right smack-dab on the day Eddy Eggby went missing! I've been researching her a lot and she's wearing the same outfit as the one she was wearing on the day she disappeared!"

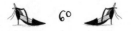

"Maybe she wore it more than once, Fluffanora . . ."

"No, Tiga! Eddy Eggby never wore the same thing more than once! She was famous for it! That hat—she only wore it once, and I remember that pattern on the dress. Her disappearance must have something to do with that evil baby!"

Tiga didn't agree, but since being adopted by the Brews she had learned that there was no use trying to change Fluffanora's mind.

"We need to go back soon," Tiga said. "I hope Felicity Bat isn't still in Clutterbucks."

"Why don't you go in disguise?" Mrs. Clutterbuck of the Past suggested.

"Yes!" Tiga and Fluffanora cried.

"But where do we get disguises?" Tiga asked, peering out the small hatch. Tiga could see a group of witches huddled outside.

"I heard she's bringing it into town to pick up Eddy Eggby," the tallest witch said.

"They say it's beyond evil. Last thing we want around here is an evil baby," another added.

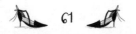

"I told you," Fluffanora hissed at Tiga.

"You don't have much time, you need to hurry," the first Mrs. Clutterbuck said as she wriggled out of her skirt. "Here, take my skirt."

Her pants were as ruffled as her skirt.

"And you can have my hat and shawl," another witch said, throwing them at Tiga.

"You'd better get back on the BOOM," Mrs. Clutterbuck said, pushing the drink into Tiga's hand. "Before it's too late."

Fluffanora held her nose and gulped it down. "One, two . . ."

BOOM!

TOAD
MAGAZINE

Inferior Fashion Followers! In today's *Toad* we will be discussing a lot of stuff about me. I was thinking of changing the name of the magazine simply to *HOOF*. Or something that combines the two names, like *Toof*. *Hoad*? *Hoofoad*? But actually I can't be bothered.

Now, NEW TREND ALERT: Wearable Cats.

It occurred to me, completely by myself and not because I saw Fluffanora do it, that we just do not take advantage of the fact that there are so many cats that we could wear.

They are soft and fluffy and have claws, so they can attach themselves to any outfit. You could, say, put one on your head, like a hat, or get a load of them to stick their claws into your legs and form a skirt shape.

Fashion is full of endless possibilities. And one of those possibilities is catwear.

I have put together some examples of how you could wear cats, modeled by me. First up, the casually cool CAT CARDIGAN.

I know, I look GREAT.

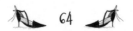

Or why not make a statement with some CAT SHOES?

Note: it's difficult to walk without the cats running away.

And now, finally, for those cold winter nights, why not go for this CATSUIT?

11

The Secret Passageway

"I can barely see!" Tiga shouted through the shawl that Fluffanora had draped over her hat.

"Shhh," Fluffanora said in her huge Mrs. Clutterbuck skirt, as she wriggled her ruffle-bottomed way down the street and through an open window at the back of the Brews' house.

Inside, Mrs. Brew's office had been ransacked. "Felicity Bat and Aggie Hoof have obviously been here looking for us," Tiga whispered, climbing over the piles of paper and fabric on the floor.

"Well, that's good. That means they won't be back," Fluffanora said.

"For now . . . ," Tiga grumbled. "Or they could still be in the house . . ."

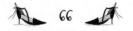

Fluffanora thought about this for a moment. "Well then, let's take the secret passageway upstairs. They won't know about that."

Mrs. Brew had had the secret passageway built so she could zoom from her office to any room in the house in an instant.

She used it mainly for zooming to the kitchen for snacks.

All you had to do was sit on the chair behind the desk and mumble, "Secret chair, secret chair, take me to YOU KNOW WHERE." And it would take you to whichever room in the house you were thinking about.

Fluffanora jumped onto the chair and Tiga squeezed in next to her. She inhaled a mouthful of fabric—the skirt was so ruffly that when smooshed on the chair, both of them could barely see over the layers and layers of fabric.

"You give the order," Fluffanora said, slapping Tiga's leg. Tiga closed her eyes, mumbled the magic words, and thought of Mrs. Brew's bedroom upstairs.

"We'll pick up some supplies and then we'll set out

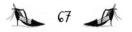

to find Peggy," Tiga said as she took off her hat and the annoying shawl.

The chair spun around. The desk moved backward and the carpet underneath it rolled up, revealing a trapdoor in the floor.

Fluffanora sighed and inspected her nails—she had taken the chair a million times. Tiga, who had only ever been shown the chair, and told *never* to use it, clung on for dear life.

The chair dived forward into the darkness and whooshed along a dark corridor.

Little lanterns lined the walls, which were decorated with hundreds of sketches of dresses.

The chair zoomed left and then right and then began moving upward, like an elevator, spinning as it went.

Tiga squeezed her eyes shut.

When she opened them again, the chair was moving quickly along another corridor. A nightgown magically appeared on top of the dress Tiga was wearing. And then some slippers magically appeared on her feet. Tiga looked up just in time to see a hairnet being lowered

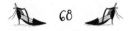

onto her head. It came down too far and stuck to her face instead.

Then a glittery powder floated down onto them.

"That's beautiful," Tiga said through the hairnet.

Fluffanora's eyes widened. "Did you think about Mom's bedroom when you got in the chair?"

Tiga nodded. "Yeah, why?"

"SHE FINDS IT DIFFICULT TO SLEEP, SO SHE MADE THAT GLITTERY STUFF TO HELP HER SL—"

"Fluffanora?" Tiga asked as Fluffanora's head lolled forward and she snorted and snored loudly.

And then everything went black.

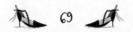

Felicity Bat Makes a Plan

M eanwhile, back at Linden House . . .

"Fel-Fel! Fel-Fel! Fel-Fel! Do you want to read my article for *Toad*, Fel-Fel? It's excellent."

Felicity Bat shoved her out of the way. "No. I'm thinking. I can't believe you lost them!"

"You did too," Aggie Hoof dared to point out.

"I'M THINKING!" Felicity Bat snapped.

"Plotting-thinking, Fel-Fel?"

"Always," Felicity Bat snapped.

"Well, I hope you're plotting-thinking very hard, because wherever Tiga and Fluffanora are hiding, it is a very hidden spot," Aggie Hoof said.

Felicity Bat clenched her fists. "They aren't going to ruin this for me. I am meant to rule Sinkville. ME!

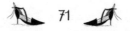

My family rules Sinkville the best—we always have and we always will. Sinkville is MINE."

"I didn't realize Sinkville was yours, but that explains why you get so angry and your face goes like that when other witches try to stop you," Aggie Hoof said airily. "I'm surprised more witches aren't on your side, considering Sinkville is *yours* . . ."

Felicity Bat stared at Aggie Hoof and then grinned.

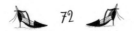

Aggie Hoof wasn't used to the grinning, so she took a nervous step backward.

"We've been wasting time looking for them when we can make the other witches do it for us!" Felicity Bat said as she flicked through *The Celia Crayfish Years*.

"But how, Fel-Fel?"

Felicity Bat cupped her hands to her mouth and started mumbling some words.

"What are you doing, Fel-Fel?"

"Starting a storm," Felicity Bat said with a cackle.

"But I HATE storms."

Outside the window on Ritzy Avenue, everything grew darker. A crack of thunder sounded as the wind picked up and thousands of bits of paper flew past, soaring fast and flapping furiously. One stuck to the window.

"Oooh," said Aggie Hoof.

WANTED. SHE'S NOT A WITCH was stamped on the paper, along with a huge picture of Tiga's face.

Aggie Hoof shook her head. "Lots of witches won't bother to read that, I never read stuff like that."

Felicity Bat smirked. "I'm not finished . . ."

She cupped her hands to her mouth again, mumbled something, and then clapped her hands once.

Aggie Hoof raised an eyebrow. "What did you just do?"

Felicity Bat said nothing.

"What did you do, Fel-Fel? Was it—" She looked down at her skirt.

"Ooh, my skirt's made of paper posters!" she squealed. ". . . OH MY FROGCAKES, FEL-FEL! DID YOU KNOW TIGA'S WANTED FOR NOT BEING A WITCH?!"

13

Dribble

Tiga and Fluffanora had been lying in a ruffled heap on the chair for an hour before something made them stir.

"Idiots," a cat hissed.

Tiga rubbed her eyes. A fuzzy ball of black fluff slowly came into view.

"Mrs. Pumpkin?" Tiga mumbled as the cat jumped onto Fluffanora and batted her face with her paw.

Fluffanora wiped some dribble off her chin. "Wha—where? DRAGONS!"

Tiga got up and steadied herself.

"Tiga, your skirt!" Fluffanora gasped. "It's made of posters!"

"Idiots," Mrs. Pumpkin hissed again.

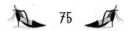

Tiga bent over and read her skirt. "It says . . . She's not . . . a . . . witch. But I *am* a witch!"

"What does the small print say?" Fluffanora asked, holding up her own skirt, also made of Felicity Bat's silly posters.

"It says she will destroy us all," Tiga grumbled.

"No, she won't! You've beaten Felicity Bat once, you'll beat her again."

"No, that's what the poster says—about me. 'Tiga Whicabim will destroy us all,'" Tiga said, slumping on the ground.

"Ah," said Fluffanora, waving her hand dismissively. "Well, that's just ridiculous. Who's going to believe that?"

"We need to find Fran," Tiga said.

Fluffanora stared at Tiga for a moment. "Or . . . maybe . . . we could, I don't know, not find Fran? She's loud. You're a wanted witch. That's a dangerous pairing if ever I heard one. Also, her glittery dust, Tiga. It gets *everywhere.*"

Tiga laughed. "No, we need Fran. I just have no idea how we're going to find her if I have to hide."

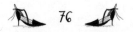

"I am as sure as a frog in the rain that good old Fran will find us," Fluffanora said as Mrs. Pumpkin wandered over to the window and meowed pointedly.

Tiga followed her and peeked outside. Over a hundred witches had already assembled on the street.

"*Psst,*" one of the witches whispered. "Maybe Tiga Whicabim's hiding in here . . ."

"They say she's the reason Peggy left," another whispered. "You can't be too near to a non-witch, it does strange things to you. She drove Peggy away!"

"Frogmuffins, this is not good," Tiga grumbled.

"I THINK I JUST SAW HER IN CAKES, PIES, AND THAT'S ABOUT IT REALLY!" a witch roared, and off they all scuttled down the road.

"You never know . . . they might not be trying to hunt you down," Fluffanora said as she peered nervously out the window at all the witches charging down the road in *SHE'S NOT A WITCH* poster skirts.

14

Tiga and Fluffanora Also Make a Plan

Tiga sat curled up on her bed as Fluffanora paced the room. Tiga's slug was peering out through the window of its little dollhouse at her. Mrs. Brew had bewitched the dollhouse so that when the slug slimed its way around, the doors to the various rooms opened for it. And the stairs moved like an escalator.

"We don't have time for this nonsense," Tiga said. "I can't believe they think I'm to blame for Peggy's disappearance. I just don't understand what could have happened to her—she could be anywhere!"

Fluffanora nodded, "Mmm, it's weird . . . She went to see Celia Crayfish and then, GONE."

"FLUFFANORA!" Tiga yelled, leaping to her feet. "Focus! We are supposed to be looking for Peggy. I

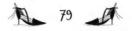

was talking about Peggy. P-E-G-G-Y. We are supposed to be looking for her. Not Eddy Eggby. Stop thinking about where Eddy Eggby disappeared to. That was hundreds of years ago."

"Only one hundred," Fluffanora corrected her. "But, yes, sorry. You're right. Peggy first."

She opened the black iron gate that surrounded her side of the room, climbed up the spiral staircase that led to her bed, and plonked herself down.

They had decided, when Tiga moved in, to share a room. Tiga's side was all neat and filled with bookshelves crammed with spell books. Her bed was a simple four-poster one, and Mrs. Brew had designed a special fabric with a slug print to hang as curtains around it.

Fluffanora's side of the room was a lot busier. She had a large traffic light that had fallen from one of the pipes years ago. When Tiga moved in, Fluffanora had removed the lights and bewitched a picture of Eddy Eggby's face into the "go" part, and a picture of a squashed frog into the "stop" part. Eddy Eggby's face meant you could enter; the squashed frog meant you could not.

Behind the traffic light was an iron fence with lots of clothes hanging off it. Beyond the iron fence, Tiga found when she was allowed inside for the first time, sat a squishy sofa and an armchair, around a little table that was magic—a hand always popped out of it holding your favorite cake. Fluffanora also had a magic teacup that refilled with tea as soon as you finished it. And she had pristine bookshelves filled with her favorite stories from when she was little.

Tiga's favorite was *Melissa's Broken Broom* by a witch named Gloria Tatty. It was Sinkville's bestselling picture book, and it was about a little girl named Melissa who kept trying to eat her broom and breaking it. Tiga's favorite chapter was the one where Melissa made an elaborate sandwich with all kinds of layers (including a broom layer!) and then tried to eat it, breaking four of her teeth.

Then you climbed a spiral staircase to Fluffanora's bed, which sat high up in the room—so high you could touch the roof when you lay down. The roof was bewitched to look like the world above the pipes.

Tiga would lie in her bed and crane her neck over the edge so she could see the buses and dogs and people running past.

Of course, it was only what Mrs. Brew imagined the world above the pipes to be, so occasionally a pigeon the size of a car would waddle past. Or someone would be flying on a vacuum cleaner.

"We have no evidence to go on. All we know is two

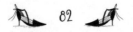

days ago Peggy was in Linden House and now she isn't," Fluffanora shouted down.

Tiga stood up and walked over to the traffic light. It changed from the squashed frog to Eddy Eggby.

"ENTER!" Fluffanora called.

Tiga walked through the iron gate, past the little table, which offered her a strawberry tart, and up the spiral staircase to Fluffanora's bed.

"I don't even know where to begin," Tiga said. She flicked her finger and a little notebook appeared in her hand, along with a pen. It started scribbling what Tiga was saying. "Peggy could be anywhere. Who knows where she went from Linden House."

Fluffanora grabbed the pen and tossed it away. "Let's just keep it simple. The last known place she was seen was Linden House, so we start there."

"How are we going to get in there without being seen?" Tiga said with a sigh.

Fluffanora jumped off her bed and slid down the spiral staircase. She flicked her finger and one of the bookcases swung open, revealing a huge walk-in closet.

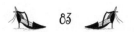

"We'll get in, Tiga, don't you worry."

Tiga followed her. "Fluffanora, there is no way we can sneak in there. It's too risky."

"We aren't going to sneak in, Tiga . . ."

"What?" Tiga said, instantly intrigued, as Fluffanora threw clothes all over the place.

"We are going straight in through the front door. All we need is a good disguise . . ."

15

Shoeland

"You're from *where*?" Aggie Hoof said, an eyebrow raised.

"Smock Alley in the distant town of . . . Shoeland," Tiga said in a sort of old-lady-who-has-just-stubbed-her-toe voice. She adjusted her disguise, pulling her hat forward over her eyes. She was wearing an outfit Fluffanora had hastily thrown together for her— a combination of one of Fluffanora's black fluffy sweaters and a DISGUSTING spotted, frilly skirt Fran had bought Tiga as a Welcome to Ritzy City, Forever! present. Fluffanora had fastened the skirt and top together with some huge black-and-white buttons. It looked outrageous.

"Shoeland . . . ," Aggie Hoof repeated.

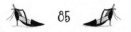

Smock Alley was in fact a real place. It was in Silver City, the next biggest city in Sinkville after Ritzy City. Mrs. Brew had studied design there when she was younger, and Fluffanora had been there once. But Shoeland was completely made up by Tiga in a moment of panic.

"You haven't heard of Shoeland?" Fluffanora bellowed in a deep and raspy voice, while shooting Tiga a look. "Why, I thought you knew everything about fashion. You are the editor of *Toad*!"

"Oh, I do, and I've definitely heard of Shoeland," Aggie Hoof insisted. "It's . . . lovely there."

"Can we come in, then?" Tiga asked. "We have many outfits for you to try on—very exclusive. No one in all of Bootland, I mean *Shoe*land, has seen them yet. And certainly no one from Ritzy City!"

Aggie Hoof giggled and leapt about on the spot. "Oh, I'll be the first to see! Is that silly skirt you're wearing going to be the next big thing?"

Fluffanora looked down at the garment she'd made by attaching teacups to her skirt and wrapping about ten glittery belts around her top. "No, this is actually

almost out of fashion now. But we have some FABULOUS new things in these boxes here . . ."

"YOU MUST COME IN!" Aggie Hoof squealed, eagerly eyeing the boxes. "I want to see EVERYTHING!"

And in the two of them went, right through the front door, just like Fluffanora had said they would.

"Shoeland. Really?! You almost blew it!" Fluffanora hissed at Tiga.

☆⭐☆

"Is your little friend here, dear?" Fluffanora asked Aggie Hoof as she nervously peered down the corridor.

Aggie Hoof might have fallen for their disguises, but Felicity Bat certainly wouldn't.

"She's out getting everything set up for the Witch Trial!" Aggie Hoof said from the screen she was changing behind. "She's going to put Tiga on trial when the townspeople find her!"

Tiga wiped a bead of sweat off her head and straightened up her wig. "We don't have time for dressing-up games," she whispered to Fluffanora.

"Oh, come on, it's hilarious," Fluffanora said as Aggie Hoof emerged from the changing room.

"So I hook the shoes over my ears?" she asked as she hooked a shoe heel over her ear. "And it's really the new fashion to wear the pants *over* your skirt?"

"Oh yes," Fluffanora said, stifling a giggle. "Now, let's make sure we get a picture."

"May I use your bathroom?" Tiga asked.

"Along the corridor," Aggie Hoof said as she pulled a pair of tights onto her head.

"So beautiful," Fluffanora said.

Tiga tore down the corridor.

"Peggy?" she hissed.

"PEGGY?"

Right, I am an evil witch and I need to hide another witch. Where do I hide her? Tiga thought.

In a cupboard!

Under a rug!

Behind a curtain!

She didn't come up with anything good!

"Pegs? Where are you?" she called as she dived in and out of rooms.

She stopped by the study. A lone lamp sat on the desk casting a warm light over a pile of papers. Tiga scuttled into the room and began riffling through them.

"I think this outfit will do. You're right, it *is* better with the pants over my skirt," she heard Aggie Hoof say. "You sure know fashion in Shoeland. And the hats on my feet, what do you call them?"

". . . Hateels," Tiga heard Fluffanora say.

The papers were useless. Tiga flicked through them, discarding them as she went. Mostly they were requests for law changes that had been sent from other witches. Just as Tiga was giving up, she spotted something. It was a small scrap of paper, but it was clearly Peggy's handwriting in the corner.

Call Miss Flint about the doll

Miss Flint was the owner of Desperate Dolls, the creepy doll shop in the Docks. Tiga stuffed the piece of paper into her pocket. It wasn't much, but maybe Miss Flint and Peggy had arranged to meet. Maybe Miss Flint had been the last person to see her.

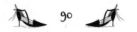

"Okay, well, we'd better be off, back to beautiful old Shoeland," Tiga heard Fluffanora say. Tiga raced down the corridor and met them just as they were walking out into the hallway.

Aggie Hoof looked like a bunch of naughty cats had tried to dress her.

"Be sure to walk around town and show off our fabulous designs!" Fluffanora said, barely able to contain her laughter.

"Oh, I will," mumbled Aggie Hoof through the stripy sock pulled over her face. " 'Bye."

TOAD MAGAZINE

It's me again, for another issue of *Toad*! I think we all know it's going to be MAGIC.

You will see I have themed this issue SHOELAND. Shoeland is a place, although it isn't on any map I've seen, so I don't know where it is, but some people from Shoeland visited me, so it definitely exists. Shoeland is full to the brim with the most wonderful fashions. I have filled the magazine with examples, all modeled by me. And IF YOU DON'T WEAR SHOELAND FASHIONS, YOU WILL BE IN SO MUCH TROUBLE, OKAY?

'Bye.

Aggie Hoof,

Editor. Co-Ruler. Shoeland fan.

16

Miss Flint

"I've told you once and I'll tell you again, I DON'T speak to them vile witches from above the pipes and I certainly ain't never speaking to a witch from Ritzy. So I ain't speaking to either of you," Miss Flint ranted.

They were in Desperate Dolls. Tiga was thinking about the first time she had visited the place, with Peggy, when they competed in Witch Wars. It seemed so long ago now. She was completely lost in thoughts of adventures with Peggy when a familiar buzzing sound butted in and disturbed her.

"What about meeee?" Fran said as she shot through the air and landed on Miss Flint's desk. There was a large doll sitting on it with an arm missing, and Miss

Flint was sticking an old doll leg on in its place. "Will you talk to meeee?"

"FRAN!" Tiga cried. She had never been so happy to see the bossy, buzzy thing.

Fran zoomed up to her face, slapped against her cheek, and gave her a sort-of face cuddle. "I've been trying to find you. Everyone has. Oh I'm so worried, little dear, I—"

"Get out, all of you," Miss Flint snapped.

"But I want to ask you something, Miss Flint," Fran said, twirling in the air and sending glittery dust shooting everywhere.

"What?" Miss Flint asked impatiently.

"What do I want to know?" Fran whispered to Tiga.

"You want to know," Tiga whispered back, "when she last saw Peggy, and if Peggy contacted her about a doll."

Fran relayed the message to Miss Flint, who shook her head. "I haven't seen or heard from Peggy for about a month. Last time I saw her, she was opening the fancy new shoe houses across the road there."

Tiga showed her Peggy's note. "So you don't know what this could mean?"

Miss Flint peered down at it and shook her head again.

No Such Place as Shoeland

"THERE'S NO SUCH PLACE AS SHOELAND," Felicity Bat said, prodding Aggie Hoof's head through the stripy sock.

"They definitely said Shoeland," she mumbled.

Felicity Bat sighed. "Well, they were definitely lying then, weren't they?"

"I don't think they were; they knew all about the fashions there . . ."

Felicity Bat crushed the dainty little teacup in her hand. "Well, at least we know they haven't left Ritzy City."

"Who?" Aggie Hoof asked.

Felicity ripped the sock off Aggie Hoof's head. "Tiga and Fluffanora, you complete IDIOT."

"OUCH!" Aggie Hoof squealed.

Felicity Bat cackled. "It's only a matter of time before we catch them, my friend."

"*Best* friend," Aggie Hoof corrected her.

18

The Witch Trial

"And did I tell you about *my hair*?" Fran asked as Tiga and Fluffanora ran along the alleyways in the Docks. "And do you know what Felicity Bat has done to Brollywood? BANNED FAIRY FIVE, the best TV station. It's hideous, just hideous!"

"Why did she do that?" Tiga asked.

"She finds fairies ANNOYING," Fran said, twirling in the air and shooting glittery dust everywhere. "*Annoying.* Can you believe it?!"

"Well . . . ," Fluffanora began, dusting herself down, but Tiga elbowed her before she could say any more.

A poster flapped on a nearby lamppost. *FIND TIGA, THE FAKE WITCH*, it read.

"That's a lovely photo of you!" Fran said, pointing at the poster.

Tiga sighed and shook her head just as something tiny shot out from behind it and darted toward her.

"STOOOP!" it squealed.

It smacked into Tiga's face. Not the face on the poster. Her real face.

"Frognails!" Tiga squealed.

"*Crispy*," Fran said through gritted teeth.

Tiga peeled the irate fairy off her nose, going cross-eyed as she tried to focus on her. "What are you *doing*, Crispy?!"

"I am arresting you!" said Crispy jubilantly.

Fran wagged a finger in Crispy's face. "I forbid it!"

Crispy took out a tiny pair of handcuffs and attached them to Tiga's finger. "Aha! Got you!"

Fluffanora rolled her eyes and watched as Crispy puffed and panted and tried to pull Tiga along the road.

"Why am I under arrest?" Tiga asked.

Crispy fumbled in her tiny pocket for something.

She pulled out a little scroll of paper. "You are under arrest for not being a witch!"

"I am a witch. When you jumble up the letters in my name, it spells 'I am a big witch,'" Tiga said flatly.

"Before I take you to Linden House, though," Crispy said quietly, "I need a very quick favor . . ."

19

Toe Pinchers

"I refuse to play any part in this!" Fran said as she floated about in the air, hands on her hips, nostrils flared.

Tiga found herself standing in the middle of a set in Brollywood. There was a curtain floating magically in front of them. It swayed slowly. Lizzie Beast was holding a small spotlight over the set. She nodded at Tiga.

Tiga smiled back.

"But *Toe Pinchers* is going to be the greatest film ever made. It will almost certainly win Best and Only Fairy Film of the Year," Crispy said to Fran. "I just need one more tiny toe pincher."

"If I do it, will you let Tiga go?" Fran said through gritted teeth.

Crispy thought for a moment.

"No. I have to turn her in."

"Why do you *have* to?" Fran asked.

"So I look really clever for catching her, of course."

Fran crossed her arms. "Well . . . that sort of makes sense. But if you are going to turn Tiga in, I have no incentive to act in *Toe Pinchers*."

"What about HER?" Crispy asked, suddenly distracted by a small thing sliming its way across the floor.

"My slug!" Tiga cried, scooping up the slug and patting its beehive of hair. "How did you get here?"

"She must have hidden in your hat," Fran said with a tut.

"She is PERFECT!" Crispy cheered.

"For *Toe Pinchers*?" Tiga asked defensively, holding the slug close to her.

Crispy nodded madly.

Just then all the fairies filed in. Tiga hadn't seen them since Witch Wars—the Sulky Sisters and Millbug-Mae and Donna and Sally and Julie Jumbo Wings (although,

technically, it's just Julie). They were all dressed in matching black dresses and looked really bored. Some of them were making noises like "*mmmmm, brrrr, aaaaah, weeeee.*"

"They're warming up," Lizzie Beast explained. "They also like to dance to music before we start filming, to loosen up." She flicked her finger, and a small box floated through the air. It looked just like a jewelry box and slowly opened to reveal a little statue of a fairy.

Lizzie Beast nodded and the tiny box started shaking furiously and blaring *really* loud music.

Tiga covered her ears.

Fluffanora groaned.

All the fairies started clapping their hands and soaring around in the air.

Glittery dust was EVERYWHERE.

"MY EYES ARE BURNING!" Fluffanora screamed.

The fairies continued to wiggle around in the air. Even the Sulky Sisters, who were usually miserable, had huge grins smacked on their faces and were shimmying across the room doing jazz hands.

"IT'S ONE OF THE SILVER RATS' NEW SONGS. IT'S CALLED 'PULL SHAPES.' THEY LOVE IT," Lizzie Beast shouted over the noise of the tiny box.

Donna the fairy swung her hair around, and Millbug-Mae danced right up to Tiga's face and clapped, sending glittery dust shooting up her nose. She sneezed, dropped the slug and, before anyone knew what was happening, *Toe Pinchers* was being filmed with the slug playing the role of the sixth fairy. Sorry, *toe pincher*.

"Right, everyone," said Crispy from her tiny director's chair. "ACTION!"

The slug inched onto the set.

Tiga was watching from behind the camera. The slug's beehive came into view. After about five minutes, because slugs move *really* slowly.

A voice-over, which sounded a lot like Crispy trying to speak in a deep voice, came on:

In this land of twisted trees and excellent fairies, there lives a mutant collection of evil things. These evil things are fast!

The slug inched a little farther into the shot.

These evil things are TERRIFYING.

The slug's beehive of hair flopped into view.

"Ridiculous," Fran said under her breath. Fluffanora was holding her nose to stop herself from laughing. Tiga just shook her head in amazement.

Two huge, fake feet were lowered into view by Lizzie Beast.

Mrs. Flufferknuckle, a very nice old lady, just thought she was out for a walk.

Lizzie Beast moved the feet.

"Mrs. Flunterbuffle is out for a walk with no shoes on, is she?" Fran asked.

"IT'S FLUFFERKNUCKLE," Crispy screeched. "And *shhh*."

But little did she know she was going to be attacked by A TOE PINCHER!

Fluffanora looked like she was about ready to burst.

The slug looked at the camera, confused.

"*Never* look at the camera," Fran muttered under her breath.

"Go on," Crispy hissed.

The slug slimed slowly up to the fake feet and then climbed onto the big toe.

THE TOE PINCHERS! THEY ATTACK!

The slug slimed all over the toe.

"It's just getting slime everywhere," Donna the fairy pointed out. "It's not even pinching one bit!"

Crispy sighed.

The slug flopped off the big toe and slimed off the set.

Fluffanora burst out laughing. "This is the least scary film of all time!"

Crispy scrunched up her face, and little streams of glittery dust shot out of her ears. "I'm taking you all to Linden House RIGHT NOW."

Tiga scooped up the slug and grabbed Fluffanora's arm. "NO, YOU'RE NOT!"

Lizzie Beast threw her an umbrella, Tiga grabbed it, flicked her finger, and before she knew it, they were flying fast toward the ceiling.

"DON'T DAMAGE THE SET! THE SET!" Crispy cried as they smashed right through the roof and out into the drizzly Brollywood air.

Oh, Fran!

"WHERE DO WE HIDE? WHAT DO WE DO? I AM IN PANIC MODE!" Fran shouted as she did a huge loop in the air, banged into Fluffanora's back, and flopped onto the floor.

"You know this place better than anyone, Fran," Tiga said encouragingly. "Where can we hide?"

Fran thought for a moment. "I know the perfect place! THIS WAAAAAY!" And then she shot off down the road toward Set Five.

COOKING FOR TINY PEOPLE, read the sign on the door.

Tiga and Fluffanora raced in and skidded to a halt.

Fran was bouncing up and down on top of a kitchen counter. It was about the size of a shoebox.

Tiga looked around the room. The chair was the size of a small mug. The cupboards were no taller than two stacked cans of beans.

"If anything," said Fluffanora, a finger raised, "this room is the opposite of hiding."

Fran looked up at them, two huge witches in a room filled with very tiny things.

Tiga tried to hide her foot behind the fridge (about the size of an upright banana) and knocked it over.

"I didn't think this through . . . ," Fran said as Crispy shot through the door and shouted, "ARRESTED!"

"Frogs," Tiga grumbled.

Fluffanora pelted out the door.

"GOT YOU!" Crispy shouted up Tiga's left nostril.

Tiga winced and glanced around the room. "Did Fluffanora *leave*?!"

"Well, my fridge is well and truly broken," said Fran.

21

The Witch Trials

All of Ritzy City stared up at Tiga, who was perched on a stand outside Linden House.

"She's not a witch!" someone cried.

"SHE'S NOT A WITCH!" the crowd chanted as Tiga stared at them all in disbelief.

"I *am* a witch!" she yelled back.

"SHE'S NOT A WITCH!" they all continued to shout.

Felicity Bat stepped onto the platform and raised a hand in the air. The crowd went silent.

"As you all know," she said firmly, "strange things have been happening in this town. Important witches have started to vanish!"

"Like Darcy Dream, the editor of *Toad*," a witch cried.

"She's not missing, she's just playing hide-and-seek with herself," Aggie Hoof said.

"Yes, well, many others have been reported missing on this very day," Felicity Bat went on, glaring at Aggie Hoof. "There have been strange noises! The town's cats have been crying!"

"People are wearing crazy clothes!" a witch from the crowd screeched, pointing at Aggie Hoof.

"It's the fashion in Shoeland, actually," Aggie Hoof corrected her.

The witch looked confused.

"The only thing that could cause all of this is a witch among us who is not a witch at all! TIGA WHICABIM!" Felicity Bat shouted, riling up the crowd.

Someone threw a shoe at Tiga's head.

"OUCH!"

"She feels pain! She's not a witch!" someone cried.

"Witches feel pain," Tiga argued.

"She SPEAKS! So she's not a witch!" another witch from the crowd yelled.

Tiga threw her hands in the air. "You've all gone mad!"

"She's not a witch—she has HANDS!" another witch yelled.

Felicity Bat was grinning a mad grin, clearly enjoying the hysteria she had whipped up.

"Non-witches can cause great trouble in Sinkville. They are to be feared! To be hated! To be HUNTED DOWN!" she said.

The crowd went wild. Someone lobbed another shoe at Tiga. This time she caught it.

"SHE CATCHES THINGS! SHE'S NOT A WITCH!"

Tiga sighed.

Fran hovered above the crowd. "Witches can catch things, and so can fairies!" she shouted.

A witch threw a shoe at Fran and knocked her out of the air.

"SHE'S NOT A WITCH!" another cried at Tiga.

Tiga spotted an elaborate hat moving around in the crowd. Witches started to whisper and pass around a piece of paper.

The hat tilted upward and Tiga could make out the face—it was Fluffanora!

She winked at Tiga.

"What evidence do you have that I'm not a witch? *Real* evidence?" Tiga demanded.

Felicity Bat cackled. "Aggie Hoof, read out the evidence!"

Aggie Hoof stepped forward and adjusted the skirt that was hanging around her neck. "Number one, you arrived in Ritzy City recently from the world above the pipes, where non-witches live."

"Where I lived with a witch called Miss Heks," Tiga responded.

"Number two," said Aggie Hoof, ignoring her. "You used to wear jeans, like non-witches."

"Because I lived above the pipes!" Tiga said, sounding exasperated.

"Number three. You do not have a cat like most witches. Your familiar is this." She held up the slug and gagged.

"Put her down!" Tiga yelled, lunging forward.

Aggie Hoof threw it onto the ground and Felicity Bat flicked her finger, sending the slug soaring high up into the air.

Tiga gasped as she watched it fall fast. Fluffanora was shuffling left and right in the crowd.

"Catch her!" Tiga yelled just as the slug slopped into Fluffanora's hand. She held it up and smiled.

"A small victory," said Felicity Bat. "But it is clear you are not a witch."

"I can do MAGIC!" Tiga shouted, flicking her finger, but nothing happened. She tapped it against her leg and tried again. She just wanted to flick off one of the witches' hats in the front of the crowd, that's all! She tried again. Nothing. She was getting better at spells, but she was terrible under pressure.

"SHE'S NOT A WITCH!" the crowd yelled. "Her finger IS USELESS!"

Felicity Bat nodded. "Exactly. Not a witch. And so you must be punished."

"Not so fast," came a voice from the crowd. It was Mavis, the witch who owned the jam stall. "According

to this, *you* are not a witch, Felicity Bat." She held up a piece of paper.

Felicity Bat grabbed it and cackled. "Well, this is obviously made up . . . by YOU," she seethed, pointing at Fluffanora.

"How could I make up a photograph?" Fluffanora said with a shrug as all the witches in the crowd began speaking in hushed voices.

Tiga peered over at the piece of paper. It was Felicity Bat, sitting smartly on a seat in her Pearl Peak Academy school uniform. On her head was a hat with big neon lights that read, *I AM NOT A WITCH*.

"She's messed with the photo and added that stupid hat," Felicity Bat said smugly, scrunching the piece of paper up into a ball.

Everyone in the crowd held a piece of paper up to her nose and examined it.

"FROGSTICKS!" Felicity Bat screeched.

"I made some copies," Fluffanora said casually.

Felicity Bat charged into the crowd. "*You!*" she seethed.

Tiga watched as Fluffanora subtly flicked her finger.

The crowd erupted into hysterical cackles!

On Felicity Bat's head, there now sat the very same hat from the photo. Only this time the light was flashing on and off: *I AM NOT A WITCH. I. AM. NOT. A. WITCH. IAMNOTAWITCH.*

Felicity Bat didn't notice until Aggie Hoof yelled, "Fel-Fel, your hat! It's saying you're not a witch lots!"

Felicity Bat tore the hat off her head and marched back into Linden House. "I'll get you, Tiga Whicabim," she hissed as the crowd cried with laughter.

The Eddy Eggby Photo

After the ridiculous trial, if you can even call it that, Felicity Bat went into hiding, clearly mortified, and completely sure she should *never* have trusted an idea inspired by something Aggie Hoof said. Aggie Hoof continued to walk around town dressed in the "Shoeland" fashions, and Tiga, Fluffanora, and Fran carried on with their search for Peggy, safe in the knowledge that nobody believed Tiga was responsible for Peggy's disappearance. But witches were still disappearing, and most of the witches—well, the good ones, anyway—wanted Felicity Bat out of Linden House. No one more so than Tiga.

She and Fluffanora, assisted with glitter and much shrieking from an enthusiastic Fran, traveled to the depths of Wavely Way, and to the tip of Pearl Peak.

They made a long list of all the places Peggy was most likely to be and were dangerously close to ticking them all off. Fluffanora had suggested that the terrible pair might have taken Peggy farther afield—to one of the other cities in Sinkville. There was Silver City, where Mrs. Brew went to college, and where most of the buildings were perched high on spindly silver stilts. And there was Driptown, but there wasn't much to see there. Most of it was underwater. Apparently, according to Fluffanora, none of the other cities were as good as Ritzy City. And they were completely empty since the Big Exit—all the witches had just left. That didn't mean that Aggie Hoof and Felicity Bat couldn't have ventured to one of the empty cities and hidden Peggy there, though . . .

Tiga lay in bed wide awake, thinking about the huge map of Sinkville painted on the wall in Linden House and how IMPOSSIBLE it was going to be to find Peggy. Her slug snoozed and slimed on the pillow next to her.

Fran had decided to sleep in the slug's little house, since it was the perfect size for her. The slug hadn't seemed happy about that. But it's always difficult to tell, because a slug doesn't really have much of a face.

Tiga couldn't understand how everyone could get to sleep so easily when Peggy was in peril. Didn't they care? What if they couldn't find her? What if Felicity Bat destroyed Sinkville and made it all evil and terrible? What if Aggie Hoof never took those shoes off her ears?

She'd had enough.

"Fluffanora?" she whispered. "Are you asleep?"

Fluffanora didn't answer. Tiga climbed out of bed and walked over to the other, much more messy side of the room.

"Fluffanora?"

The traffic light showed the squashed frog. But that didn't stop Tiga. She pushed the iron gate open.

Fluffanora was sitting on her sofa, surrounded by piles of paper, a single light dancing above them.

"Fluffanora," she whispered, "I can't sleep. I'm so worried about Peg—" Tiga stopped dead in her tracks when she saw what Fluffanora was looking at. "WHAT ARE YOU DOING?"

The hand shot up from the table, producing another strawberry tart for Tiga and knocking the papers everywhere.

"FROGLUMPS!" Fluffanora cried as the papers soared through the air.

"*Shhh*," Tiga hissed. "You'll wake up the whole house!"

Mrs. Pumpkin was curled up next to Fluffanora on the sofa. "Idiots," she hissed.

"There's no one here, apart from Fran!" Fluffanora said. "And the slug. And *this* old thing."

Mrs. Pumpkin shook her head and fell back asleep.

"I just want to know what happened!" Fluffanora said. "Is that terrible?"

Tiga took a seat next to Fluffanora and picked up one of the photos. They were all of Eddy Eggby.

"Why do you care so much about Eddy Eggby disappearing all those years ago when *Peggy* is missing right now?"

Fluffanora slumped on her sofa and looked guilty. "Well, I love Eddy Eggby."

Tiga glared at her.

"...and Peggy, of *course*. It's just I have a feeling solving the Eddy Eggby case might help us find Peggy."

"That's ridiculous," said Tiga, casually riffling through all the bits of paper. Fluffanora had collected so many things belonging to Eddy Eggby—her old notebooks; various receipts, including a handwritten one from Clutterbucks from over a hundred years ago; and notes on where she had been in the lead-up to her disappearance. She'd even found a bunch of photos.

Fluffanora picked up one of the photos and sighed. "You're right—this is nonsense. Eddy Eggby can wait."

But something in the photo caught Tiga's eye. "What have you found out?"

"Not much," Fluffanora said. "On the day Eddy Eggby disappeared, she woke up and traveled straight to Clutterbucks for her morning drink. That's when we saw her. She was planning a trip above the pipes—that's what her diary said too. She had found a pipe that led straight into the Queen of England's bathroom! She was going to look at royal fashions. Like she mentioned to us in Clutterbucks, she made a quick stop to visit Celia

Crayfish on her first birthday. And then the trail runs cold. No one saw her leave the Crayfishes' house after the visit, so no one knows if she did. There is a chance she was captured above the pipes—it was a risky trip sneaking into the queen's bathroom."

"When was that taken?" Tiga asked, pointing at the photo Fluffanora was still holding. It showed Eddy Eggby posing in front of Ritzy Avenue and waving. A jubilant crowd was standing behind her, smiling and cheering.

"It was taken along the road from Clutterbucks, right before she went to see Celia Crayfish, not long after we saw her."

Tiga took the photo and stared at it.

"I'll get rid of all this stuff. It's distracting me from finding Peggy, I know," Fluffanora said, tidying all the papers away.

But Tiga wasn't paying attention. She had spotted the most peculiar thing. Two faces in the photo looked all too familiar. It was Miss Heks standing behind Eddy Eggby! Her face was half concealed and if Tiga didn't know it so well, she might not have noticed her at all. Next to Miss Heks stood old Miss Flint, the owner of Desperate Dolls. They both looked a little less wrinkly, but not much.

"What are you looking at?" Fluffanora asked.

Tiga pointed. Miss Flint wasn't just standing there. She was slipping an old doll into Eddy Eggby's bag.

"A doll! And Peggy mentioned a doll in that note you found in Linden House!" Fluffanora cried.

"Why would Miss Flint be doing that?" Tiga asked, just as Fran flew into the bookcase, wearing an eye mask.

"Ouch!" she squealed as glittery dust exploded everywhere.

"No one told me we were having a midnight feast!" she cried as she removed the mask and spotted the strawberry tart slopped on the floor.

"We're not," Tiga and Fluffanora said flatly.

". . . You should be," Fran said, twirling in the air and sending small cakes shooting about the room. They landed in a neat pile on the floor. "Dig in," she said as a teapot zoomed around them, pouring tea into tiny little cups.

Fluffanora told Fran about the photo.

"I don't see why this is relevant!" Fran protested as her wings got caught in her puffy skirt and she crash-landed in the pot of tea.

Fluffanora fished her out and shook her.

125

"You don't think it's weird that Miss Flint slipped a doll into Eddy's bag moments before she went missing, and a hundred years later Peggy wrote a note about talking to Miss Flint about a doll and then went missing?" asked Tiga.

Fran shook her head. "Miss Flint is the owner of Desperate Dolls—dolls are probably all anyone speaks to her about."

Tiga sighed. Fran had a point.

"But Miss Flint is a weird one . . . ," Fran added.

"Maybe we can ask the Coves witches when we go there to look for Peggy!" Fluffanora suggested. "Maybe they will know something. They are the oldest witches in Sinkville, after all."

Mrs. Pumpkin's head shot up and she clawed at Fluffanora.

"NO, MRS. PUMPKIN, YOU ARE NOT COMING TO THE COVES WITH US. You will stay here, guard the house, and look after the slug."

They could see the slug, all the way across the room in the dollhouse, sliming its way up the automatic escalator stairs and heading straight for the cupboard. That was always where it hid when left alone with Mrs. Pumpkin.

"The Coves witches are far too busy partying and eating cake to know *anything*," Fran said as she licked the tea off her skirt.

"At least Felicity Bat and Aggie Hoof don't seem to be after us anymore," Tiga said. "That's *something*."

Fran wiggled on the spot, because deep down in her glittery little bones, she knew it was highly unlikely that Felicity Bat was up to nothing . . .

23

The Mmmf

Felicity Bat was standing in the foyer of a large and incredibly untidy building.

Papers and small books were stacked high like pancakes that an entire country had forgotten, and the tiny windows that lined the walls struggled to shine even the tiniest beam of light past the piles of clutter.

They were in the Mmmf, otherwise known as the Ministry of Mess and Many Files.

It was home to all of Sinkville's official documents and sat proudly in the center of Pearl Peak. Celia Crayfish had built it to keep track of all the witches of Sinkville, but since her reign as Top Witch had ended, it had become a dumping ground for any old paper or Sinkville file. No one really visited the place.

"Fel-Fel, why are we here?" Aggie Hoof moaned. "This is the number one most boring place in the one hundred most boring places to be in the top ten most boring places OF ALL TIME."

An old woman with legs as rickety as a tired chair came clattering down the spiral staircase in the middle of the room.

"Tina Gloop at your service," she said eagerly as she took a seat in front of them. They were the first visitors in years.

Since Crinkle Cauldrons had closed down, Tina Gloop, who had owned the place, had taken a job at the Mmmf to keep herself busy. It wasn't the same as the old cauldron factory—there were not nearly enough crinkles in the place for her liking. But it was something to do.

"We need everything you have on Tiga Whicabim," Felicity Bat said.

Tina Gloop raised a bushy eyebrow. "The Witch Wars girl?"

Felicity Bat nodded. "We want anything and

everything you've got." She plunked a cauldron of sinkels down in front of her.

The cauldron had a crinkled handle.

"Oh, you use Crinkle cauldrons!" Tina Gloop said with a grin so large you could have slotted the cauldron into it.

Felicity Bat nodded enthusiastically, a fake grin smacked on her face. "Oh yes! I LOVE them."

Tina Gloop chuckled and waved her spindly arms in the air. A huge black book came careering down the stairs and landed in front of them.

Aggie Hoof nearly choked on the dust.

"*Ceeeebuuuuuch*," was kind of the noise she made.

"Surname again, please," Tina Gloop said.

"Whicabim," Felicity Bat repeated.

Tina Gloop's eyes darted from side to side as the book magically flicked its own pages. After a couple of minutes, it got to the end and she turned it around and flicked through it again, this time by hand.

When she finished, she slowly raised her head and stared at them blankly.

"What have you found?" Felicity Bat demanded.

Tina Gloop slowly removed her glasses and placed them on top of the book.

"It's the strangest thing," she said slowly. "Never, in the whole history of the world below the pipes, has there ever been a witch called Whicabim."

"What does that mean, Fel-Fel?" Aggie Hoof asked. "Does that mean Tiga's not a witch?!"

Felicity Bat took the sock off Aggie Hoof's ear and smacked her with it. "No, you idiot! We made that up, remember? Tiga can do magic. I mean, she's terrible at it. Her spells during Witch Wars were awful. But she is definitely a witch."

Tina Gloop was staring at the pair of them like they were talking in Froggish (the official frog language).

"So, why are there no witches with her name, Fel-Fel?" Aggie Hoof said, sounding more confused than ever.

"Because," Felicity Bat said with a smirk, "it must not be her real name. All the time she's been asking people if they know a Whicabim, trying to figure out who she is, but no one knows a Whicabim because Whicabim is a stupid name that doesn't actually exist! She must be called something else . . ."

"But she said that was her name, Fel-Fel," Aggie Hoof went on.

"She doesn't know," Felicity Bat said with a satisfied cackle. "She doesn't even know who she is."

"But if she isn't a Whicabim, then what is she?" Aggie Hoof asked.

Felicity Bat levitated high up in the air and soared toward the door. "That is what I'm going to find out . . . with a little help from a certain small friend . . ."

"Who, Fel-Fel? I'm your best and only friend!" Aggie Hoof shouted as she trotted after her.

24

Party at the Coves

"Wheeeeeeeee!" a witch shouted as she roller-skated across the room and landed face-first in a cake.

Tiga had seen it all before. The house in the Coves was filled to the brim with witches who loved to party. The old Docks legend was that no witch ever returned from the Coves because the Coves witches were evil and probably ate other witches, but really it was because they were all having an amazing party and no one ever wanted to leave.

Fluffanora had rowed the boat out to the Coves while Fran soared above them, lighting the way with a glowing skirt. The Coves witches had seen them coming a mile off.

"Tiga, my precious bundle of above-the-pipe wonderfulness!" Bettie Cranberry said as she pelted toward them. She lifted Tiga up off the ground and swirled her around.

Lily Cranberry, a much older witch, struggled to get out of her armchair. "Tiga," she said. "So wonderful you're here again. You can turn your skirt off now, Fran."

Fran nodded her head and the bright light from her skirt faded.

"Cake?" a witch asked, slapping a piece of cake on Tiga's cheek. Tiga scraped it off and shoved it into her mouth.

The only new addition, apart from a couple of new witches, was a massive painting of Peggy. They had

re-created the picture of Peggy that had hung outside Linden House on the Witch Wars flag. She had a big swollen eye and messy hair.

"I love her," a witch said, pointing at the painting. "Is she back yet? I hear she went away to eat some fairies and has put a gigantic witch-eating bat in charge until she gets back."

"That isn't *quite* right," Tiga said.

The witch nodded knowingly. "By the time news reaches us at the Coves, it's often a little muddled."

"She's missing," Tiga explained. "Felicity Bat says Peggy put her in charge because she was 'going away with the fairies,' but we don't believe her."

"Oh, goodness! *Felicity* Bat?!" the witch cried. "I thought it was only a gigantic witch-eating bat, but this is *much* worse."

Fluffanora stepped forward. "I'm Fluffanora Brew. Lovely to meet you all."

"Ah, Fluffanora!" Lily said with a toothless smile. "I heard you are quite the brat."

"I. AM. NOOOOOT!" Fluffanora shouted.

Lily laughed. "I also heard you did a very kind thing and saved our Tiga here and brought her back to Ritzy City," she said.

Fluffanora was confused. ". . . I, well, I suppose I did."

"A brat wouldn't think to think about others. They wouldn't care to care. But you do. You aren't a real brat at all, are you?"

Fluffanora shrugged. A witch skated up to her and slapped some cake on her face, then rolled away.

"So what brings you witches here? It's not to stay, is it? Because we'll have to build more house again to accommodate you," Bettie said, sounding worried.

"We're looking for Peggy," Tiga said, pointing at the painting. "You haven't seen her, have you?"

"No, sadly not. She hasn't been to see us in a while," Bettie said.

Fluffanora took a seat next to Lily Cranberry and pulled the picture of Eddy Eggby out of her pocket.

"We sneaked into Linden House to try to find out what happened to Peggy," Tiga explained.

"And what did you find?" Bettie asked eagerly.

138

"Nothing," Tiga said. "Well, not nothing, just nothing much. I found this piece of paper. It's a note Peggy had obviously written to herself; it just says to call Miss Flint about the doll."

"What doll?" asked Bettie.

Fluffanora and Tiga shrugged.

"But while all this has been happening," Fluffanora went on, "I have been trying to figure out what happened to Eddy Eggby. We drank some BOOM and went back to Clutterbucks one hundred years ago and saw her."

"Oh, no one knows what happened to her, dear," Bettie Cranberry said. "She disappeared a long time ago."

"I found this," Fluffanora said, handing the photograph to Lily. "It shows Eddy Eggby on the day she went missing. She's standing on Ritzy Avenue. But look there in the background. Miss Flint is putting a doll in her bag."

"So she is!" said Bettie.

"We thought, given the photo and the note Peggy wrote, that perhaps Miss Flint has something to do with both disappearances," Tiga said.

Lily Cranberry was being very quiet. She just stared at the photo and smiled a sad smile. "It was better with old Eddy around," she finally said.

"Do you know Miss Flint?" Tiga asked.

Lily Cranberry looked up. "Oh yes, of course. Everyone knows Miss Flint. Although, since she was a child she has been a quiet type. I doubt you'll find anyone who knows her very well."

"I knew her very well," a spindly old witch said, stepping forward. "I was her assistant in Desperate Dolls for many years. Many, many years."

Fluffanora patted the seat next to her and the witch sat down.

"One day, I had had enough. I left the shop, jumped in a boat, and sailed to the Coves, hoping to never return and knowing that whatever terrible thing awaited me, it couldn't be as bad as old Miss Flint. Life in the shop was so boring and she barely spoke to me. Also, her cat Fuzzscrumple attacked me every morning! And what I found here wasn't bad at all," she said, looking around the room. "In fact, it was absolutely brilliant!"

"WOO-HOO!" all the witches in the room cheered, and then dissolved into a chorus of wheezy cackles again.

"Miss Flint has a routine, you know," said the old witch. "It's been the same for a long time. Every morning she gets up and rubs each of her toes individually. Then she slips on her shoes. They have a very high heel. She wears them to look taller and scarier, I think. Her dress is always the same—it's the one she bought on the day she opened up Desperate Dolls. It was the best day of her life, and she fears that if she loses the dress or one day wears another, something will happen to her beloved shop. She's very superstitious, you see. Then she stomps downstairs, always missing the last step, and walks to the kitchen, where she eats one jar of moldy jam and lets old Fuzzscrumple lick the jar."

Fluffanora shuddered.

"After breakfast, she walks sixteen steps along the road to Desperate Dolls. She opens up the shop, turns on the light, and then takes her place behind her desk. She gets to work fixing the dolls that she's piled up the night before.

"At lunchtime she goes and picks up Fuzzscrumple and the pair of them go to Nibblers, the sandwich shop in the Docks. She always has an Old Bat wrap, and Fuzzscrumple usually just licks the grime off the floor. Then they return to Desperate Dolls and she fixes the remainder of her dolls. She then takes more dolls from the big pile she has collected and plunks them on the table, ready for the next day.

"She does this every day, except for Wednesdays when she goes around Sinkville collecting old dolls. But apart from Wednesdays, her routine stays the same."

"Fascinating stuff!" Fran said, twirling in the air.

Tiga and Fluffanora nodded. It was interesting, but it didn't tell them anything particularly useful.

"One thing no witch knows," the witch added, "well, apart from me, is that every evening she puts on a huge hat and large glasses to disguise herself, and she goes to Cakes, Pies, and That's About It Really for a tart."

"But Miss Flint once told me she hates Ritzy City!" Tiga cried.

The witch nodded. "Oh, she does. But she loves those tarts."

Again, it was interesting, but it still wasn't particularly useful.

"Thank you," Tiga said. "And you don't know what Peggy could have meant about the doll? Or why Miss Flint was slipping a doll into Eddy Eggby's bag in that photo?"

The witch shook her head. "It's very strange. I doubt Miss Flint would give someone a doll for nothing, especially not a Ritzy City witch like Eddy Eggby."

"What do you think happened to Eddy Eggby?" Fluffanora asked Lily Cranberry.

"The Queen of England ate her," Lily Cranberry said matter-of-factly.

25

The Fairy Trailer Park

Felicity Bat floated into the Fairy Trailer Park, closely followed by a panting Aggie Hoof.

It was perfectly quiet, apart from the occasional squeak from the trailers that hung in the trees, swaying back and forth gently in the breeze. It was dark and the little sparkly lights from the windows glowed brightly.

"Fel-Fel! Either you need to levitate SLOWER or you need to give me a lift. I feel like my feet are going to fall off."

"Oh dear," said Felicity Bat mockingly. "If your feet fell off, where would you put your shoes?"

"Probably on my ears," Aggie Hoof said. "Like they do in Shoeland."

Felicity Bat clenched her fists, ready to argue that there WAS NO SHOELAND. But something distracted her. A fairy shot out of one of the trailers hanging on a nearby tree.

"YOU!" Felicity Bat shouted, pointing at the fairy.

"Oh, um . . . I . . . ," Crispy sighed. She slowly side-stepped in the air, trying to sneak back into her trailer.

Her trailer was the most bashed up of them all—many of them were perfect, with shiny doors and little plant pots outside. Crispy's looked like it had been stood upon. The windows were broken and the door was hanging off its hinges.

"I need you to do one more thing for me," Felicity Bat said.

Crispy sighed. "No. I already found Tiga. And I'm not your personal fairy."

Felicity Bat flicked her finger and Crispy crashed to the ground.

She winced and rubbed her elbow. "Mean," she grumbled.

Felicity Bat nodded at Crispy's trailer.

"No!" Crispy cried, shooting into the air. "*Please*, Felicity."

But it was too late. The trailer twisted and turned, and before Crispy could say "FROGLUMPS!" the trailer was sparkling new. It had a glittery door and some beautiful frilly curtains, and it was so shiny and bright that all the fairies who were peeking out of their trailers had to put on sunglasses.

"What have you done?!" Crispy cried. "You MONSTER!"

"Shall I add some pretty flowers too?" Felicity Bat asked.

Crispy shook her head frantically. "No, no, please stop. I'll do anything. ANYTHING!"

Felicity Bat snaked toward her and said quietly, "You will go to the Mmmf and look through all the files. Every. Single. One. You are looking for any document that mentions witches named Tiga. Any Tigas who might be about nine years old now."

"Like Tiga Whicabim?" Crispy asked.

"Forget the surname," Felicity Bat said with a smile. "Just look for witches named Tiga."

Following Miss Flint

Back at the Docks, Tiga and Fluffanora noticed that every witch was—somewhat reluctantly—dressed like an idiot.

"It's the fashion in the faraway Shoeland, wherever that is, and we have to wear it because Aggie Hoof said so," a witch grumbled as she adjusted the socks on her ears.

Fluffanora laughed and strapped her hat to her waist, took off a shoe and dangled it on her ear, and pulled her skirt up around her neck.

"What?" she said, smiling at Tiga. "We'd better wear the Shoeland fashions; it's the law."

Tiga flicked her finger and her tights shot off her legs and landed on her head. "Happy?" she asked Fluffanora through gritted teeth.

Fluffanora roared with laughter.

"As much as I would very much like to play a vital part in this plan of yours, I'm afraid I will have to leave you for a bit, as I need to film *Cooking for Tiny People*. I just cannot let my fans down. There would be an UPROAR!" Fran prattled on.

Tiga nodded. "We understand, Fran."

"I shall be back as soon as I can!" she cried, shooting off down the street.

"NO RUSH!" Fluffanora shouted after her.

Their plan was to follow Miss Flint's every move and look out for anything unusual, anything that might give them a clue to Peggy's whereabouts. It was Thursday lunchtime, and just like the old witch had said, Miss Flint was in Nibblers, eating an Old Bat wrap. Her cat—the scrawniest, evilest thing Tiga had ever clamped her eyes on—was standing stiffly by her leg . . .

Four hours later, Tiga yawned as they sat curled up outside the shop, peering in the window at Miss Flint stuffing eyeballs back on the dolls, or chopping their hair, or sticking on toes. The dim light in the window glowed half-heartedly as the shadows of dolls danced around inside, along with a gigantic shadow of Miss Flint and her crooked old nose.

"She's just carrying on as normal," Tiga whispered to Fluffanora, who looked really disappointed.

"Maybe she has nothing to do with it," said Fluffanora. "Maybe Peggy just wanted to buy a doll from her, Tiga."

That evening, Miss Flint closed up her shop and took the sixteen steps back to her house, accompanied by Fuzzscrumple.

Tiga and Fluffanora waited around the corner and picked at some sandwiches they'd bought from Nibblers.

"I actually don't mind this," Fluffanora said. "What's this green stuff?"

"Mold," said Tiga.

"BLEUGH!" said Fluffanora, spitting it out.

Tiga peeked around the corner and down the main street in the Docks. Peggy had done such a

 160

good job of making it better. The shoe houses looked brilliant.

"WE ARE HERE TO TAKE YOUR SHOE HOUSES!" a very familiar voice yelled.

"It's not . . . is it?" Fluffanora asked.

Tiga watched as Aggie Hoof and a levitating Felicity Bat glided down the Docks, flicking their fingers and making the shoe houses disappear.

"But that's my home!" a witch cried as her shoe house vanished and all her things—sofas, bookshelves, curtains—landed with a thud on top of her.

"I hope my cat didn't disappear too!" another cried.

"It did," said Felicity Bat with a smirk.

"Quick," Tiga whispered. "We need to move."

Felicity Bat was levitating dangerously close to the corner where Tiga and Fluffanora were hiding. She paused and sniffed the air.

"Quick," Tiga hissed, grabbing Fluffanora's arm.

They dived into the closest door to them, and fell straight into something awful.

Tiga bobbed up and down in the gloopy liquid.

 151

"This is where all the moldy jam goes to be made into cat food," Tiga said flatly. She placed a hand over Fluffanora's face so Felicity Bat couldn't hear the scream.

Suspicious...

A couple more hours passed and still nothing. Felicity Bat and Aggie Hoof, after destroying all the great shoe houses Peggy had made, had retreated to Linden House. Tiga was almost asleep by the time Miss Flint's front door creaked open, and just like the witch at the Coves had said she would, Miss Flint marched out of the Docks and straight toward Ritzy City, disguised in a big hat and a pair of glasses.

Tiga and Fluffanora scuttled along behind her, at enough of a distance not to arouse suspicion. At one point Miss Flint looked around and stared at them. They were still fairly covered in moldy jam, only now it had hardened a bit, so they looked like witches coated in some sort of horrendous crust. Fluffanora put on her

Shoeland accent and said to Tiga, "I am very excited to visit Ritzy City for the first time. Oh yes. Also, did you know it is bad luck to look backward? Terrible things can happen to you and your shop."

Miss Flint's eyes widened and she quickly turned around. She was clearly as superstitious as the Coves witch had said . . .

When they got to Ritzy City, Miss Flint went straight to Cakes, Pies, and That's About It Really and got a tart. Tiga and Fluffanora waited outside; they decided it was better than going in, in case they bumped into anyone they knew. Cakes, Pies, and That's About It Really had become one of Tiga's favorite places to hang out in Ritzy City.

Miss Flint polished off her tart.

"She's coming," Fluffanora hissed. Tiga straightened up and pretended to be chatting with Fluffanora as the old bat stomped past.

But she didn't stomp back to the Docks, like the witch in the Coves had said she would. They followed her in amazement as she went somewhere else entirely . . .

"Linden House?!" Tiga cried.

28

The Bag

Miss Flint was greeted at the door of Linden House by Aggie Hoof, who gave her a massive sack of something. Felicity Bat peeked out the door and looked around nervously like a witch doing something naughty.

"Be here at the same time tomorrow, same thing, Miss Flint," she said. Miss Flint nodded and off she went.

"Same time tomorrow," Tiga repeated. "Same thing . . ."

Just as Tiga and Fluffanora were about to follow Miss Flint back to the Docks, Tiga spotted something crazy.

"Is that . . . ?" she said, pointing at a huge pile of papers flying wonkily down the street.

The pile of papers came to a halt next to Felicity Bat and landed with a thud at her feet. That's when Tiga saw who had been carrying them—a ridiculously dusty Crispy.

"Where has she been?!" Fran cried, appearing with a pop beside them.

"Shhh," Tiga said, stepping back into the shadows as Crispy, Felicity Bat, and Aggie Hoof looked suspiciously across the road.

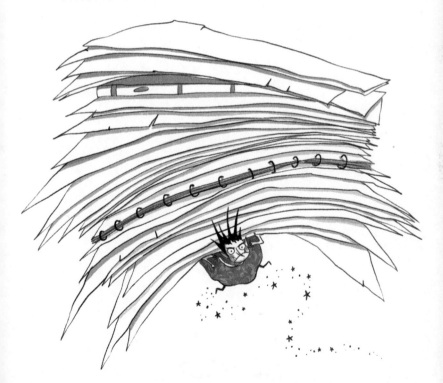

"She's covered in dust! And not the glittery, wonderful kind!" Fran prattled on.

"Perfect," they heard Felicity Bat say as she flicked through the papers.

"Can I go now?" Crispy asked, shaking the dust out of her hair.

Felicity Bat nodded. "Yes. Excellent work, my little fairy."

Crispy growled and shot off down the road.

29

Fluffanora's Shoe

Tiga and Fluffanora followed Miss Flint all the way back to her house, but she slammed her door before they could get close enough to the bag to even guess what was in it.

They slept in Fluffanora's shoe that night, just on the outskirts of the Docks. It was the fanciest shoe Tiga had ever slept in. It had ten floors and lots of winding corridors. Tiga got lost about five times. It even had a little room in it that was a smaller version of Clutterbucks.

As they had a Clutterbucks, they curled up on their floating chairs and tried to make a plan.

"What do you think those dusty old papers were?" Tiga asked.

Fluffanora shrugged. "Probably more ideas for evil

rule changes. Who cares? We need to stay focused on our mission: find out what was in that bag Felicity handed Miss Flint."

"Yes, I suppose that's all we can do . . . ," Tiga said. She was distracted. Peggy had been missing for a really long time now. What if she wasn't okay? What if, like Eddy Eggby, she vanished forever? What if *the queen* had eaten her?

"In a few hours, when she's definitely asleep, we'll sneak into Miss Flint's house and find out what's in the bag," Fluffanora said, raising her glass.

Tiga clinked her glass against it and looked at the empty seat hovering at their table.

She missed Peggy a lot.

Fran zoomed into the room and plunked herself down on the empty chair. "Well, thank you very much for waiting for me! I've been zooming around corridor after corridor looking for you. Oooh, Clutterbucks! I'll have one of their new Peggy Pigwiggle Punch drinks, please!"

Tiga glared at her.

"What?" Fran said. "I'm sure wherever Peggy is, she's delighted I'm drinking it."

Felicity Bat
Figures It Out

"I've found her!" Felicity Bat said with a cackle. "I was right, her surname isn't Whicabim at all. Not even close."

"You're brilliant, Fel-Fel," said Aggie Hoof.

Felicity Bat bowed. "I now know exactly where Tiga comes from. And I know who her mom is."

"Oooh, is it the old cart witch lady?" Aggie Hoof guessed.

"No," said Felicity Bat.

"Is it Miss Flint?"

"No," said Felicity Bat.

"Is it . . . you, Fel-Fel?"

Felicity Bat sighed. "I am *NINE*."

Aggie Hoof thought for a moment. "It's not me, is it?"

31

Inside Miss Flint's House

"It's not here!" Fluffanora hissed.

Tiga held a shaky finger up to her lips and with her other hand pointed frantically at a snoring and snorting Miss Flint.

They had managed to get into her house—through Fuzzscrumple's far-too-large cat door. Fran was downstairs in the kitchen distracting the grumpy old cat. He was jumping around pathetically on his frail, bony legs, trying to swat at her.

"Ha! You missed!" Fran said gleefully as Fuzzscrumple nearly took out one of her eyes with his claw.

Miss Flint's house was as ramshackle as her shop. And it was also filled with dolls. They lined the edges of her bedroom, hung off the top of her wardrobe, and slumped next to the table by her bed. Tiga stared at them. Their matted hair was caked in dust, their little dresses were peppered with holes, and their faces had a look that said, "This is gross, isn't it?" Miss Flint's beloved dress was hanging on the wardrobe door.

Tiga and Fluffanora crept around the room, slowly lifting up dusty dolls and peering in half-open battered drawers.

Miss Flint rolled over and grunted.

They hit the floor!

And that's when Tiga saw it, sticking out from under the bed. She pointed frantically at the bag. Fluffanora grinned.

Tiga tried to reach it, but Miss Flint snorted again, and this time rolled over, her wrinkly old arm flopping forward, blocking the bag.

Tiga tried to edge closer but Fluffanora pulled at her skirt. She shook her head and pointed at Tiga's finger.

Tiga looked blankly at Fluffanora.

"Use *magic*, you idiot," she whispered.

Tiga stared at her finger and then at the bag. Fluffanora was right, she did *have* magic, it's just she wasn't sure it was good enough. What if she accidentally did some ridiculous spell and woke Miss Flint up?

Fluffanora prodded her.

Miss Flint snored.

Tiga thought for a moment. What spell to use . . . "Aha," she whispered. "I know which one to do . . ."

It was an old spell Mrs. Brew had taught her when she was trying to reach a book on the very top shelf of Mrs. Brew's library in their house on the Cauldron Islands. "You can do many things to get it," she'd told Tiga. "You can bewitch that ladder over there to grow bigger, or you can do a simple spell to move the book toward you."

Tiga pointed her finger and mumbled the words Mrs. Brew had taught her. "Cats and frogs and rats with beards. Brooms and capes and, um, things called feards. Make this thing work."

Tiga stared at the bag.

Fluffanora had her head in her hands. The bag wasn't moving, but something else was. Miss Flint's arm began to wobble. Just a little at first, but before long it was wobbling like petrified jelly. Bigger it grew, and fatter, until it was more than double the size of Miss Flint's body. A gigantic finger, almost as tall as Tiga, flopped in front of Fluffanora.

"Uh-oh," Tiga whispered. "I think that was the spell for making the ladder bigger. What I meant to say was, *Come to me, my pretty.*"

The bag shot out from under the bed and straight into Tiga's hand.

Fluffanora, still covering her face with one hand, flicked her finger and Miss Flint's arm started to shrink back down to its normal size.

Tiga peered eagerly inside the bag.

Fluffanora mouthed, "What's inside?"

Tiga reached a hand in. Then another. Then she stuck her whole head in because something was very wrong.

"It's completely empty!" she hissed.

Fluffanora grabbed the bag and peered inside. It was indeed completely empty.

Miss Flint snorted and rolled over again.

Tiga peered under the bed. About fifty identical bags were under there. She hastily crawled under and started riffling through them all. They were all completely empty!

"They're empty. What now?" Tiga whispered to Fluffanora from under the bed. She wiped her palms on her skirt—they were all sweaty and scared.

Fluffanora got up and tiptoed toward the door. "Let's go. There's nothing here that can help us."

But Tiga spotted something. "Fluffanora," she whispered, "the dress."

Fluffanora stared at it and mouthed, "What about it?"

Tiga got to her feet, scuttled over to the wardrobe, and gently slipped the dress off its hanger.

Fluffanora stared from Tiga to Miss Flint and back again. "Huh?" she whispered.

Tiga didn't have time to explain. "It's her beloved lucky dress."

She shot out of the bedroom and down the stairs, found a piece of paper, and scribbled,

If you ever want to see your beloved dress again, come to Pearl Peak at 7:00 p.m. tomorrow. Meet me by the roller coaster and don't be late.

32

The Dress Plan

It was a brilliant plan, if Tiga did say so herself. And she did, about seventy-six times the next day.

Miss Flint would find her dress missing in the morning and, if the witch at the Coves was right, she would panic—it was her special dress and she was terrified of losing it. She would then find the note and set off to Pearl Peak to get the dress back at 7:00 p.m. That would buy Tiga and Fluffanora plenty of time to sneak into her house once more through Fuzzscrumple's cat door and get her shoes, hat, and big glasses. Tiga would put the disguise on, along with the dress, and go to Linden House and pick up the bag herself.

☆⭐☆

"FUZZSCRUMPLE, YOU COMPLETE PAIN!" Fluffanora roared as she wrestled with the cat on the kitchen floor.

Tiga slipped her feet into Miss Flint's heels and wobbled around a bit. She stomped up and down the room getting her balance. She added the hat and the glasses and she was ready to go!

Tiga marched into the kitchen and Fuzzscrumple immediately detached himself from Fluffanora's face, scuttled up to Tiga, and lovingly rubbed against her leg.

"Well, we fooled the old cat," Tiga said with a smile.

Fluffanora grinned.

☆⭐☆

"Evening, Miss Flint," Aggie Hoof said to Tiga.

Fluffanora had assured Tiga that if the disguise fooled an old, half-blind cat, it would definitely fool Aggie Hoof.

And it did.

Tiga stared at Aggie Hoof through Miss Flint's bottle-thick glasses. She wasn't sure if it was the glasses, but Aggie Hoof's face looked like it was painted silver.

"Here you go!" Aggie Hoof said, handing Tiga the bag. "I've been busy writing my article for *Toad* magazine today. I know you hate the Shoeland fashions, but would you just wear your shoes on your head, for meee? I let Felicity Bat get away with not doing it because"—she lowered her voice to a whisper—"she's scary."

Tiga grunted.

"But you, Miss Flint, would look wonderful in Shoeland fashions."

Tiga flicked her finger and sent the shoes sailing from her feet to her hat, where they perched perfectly. She had been dying to take them off anyway.

Aggie Hoof squealed and clapped.

Tiga heard a noise in the corridor.

"Is that old Miss Flint?" Felicity Bat asked.

Aggie Hoof nodded. "It is!"

Tiga spun around and hurried off down the street, clutching the bag as tightly as she could.

She rounded the corner and crashed straight into Fluffanora.

"Did you get it?" Fluffanora asked eagerly.

Tiga nodded and gasped for air. Slowly she opened the bag.

"Well, shine my glittery shoes, that is NOT what I expected!" Fran cried.

TOAD MAGAZINE

It's ME! And this time in *Toad* I have painted myself silver for my very special and evil guests, the Silver Rats!

For those of you who don't know them (Shame. On. You.), the Silver Rats are the most incredible band to ever magic up music in Sinkville. Their first album, *Glitter Grooves*, won no awards and made some people angry. And their bestselling track, "I Want to Curse Your Loved Ones," cursed some people's loved ones!

There are three of them (I think they need a fourth member and should include me, but Big Ratty, the one who does all the singing, said no). So there is Big Ratty, who does all the singing and makes bad choices for her band. Then there is Tails, who is on the decks, and Jam Jar, who plays an invisible violin thing.

They won't let magazines write their real names, which is weird because I think Lydia Claw, Gemma Gray, and Annie Legs are perfectly cool names. Apparently, Lydia Claw, Gemma Gray, and Annie Legs get really annoyed if they read an article that has their real names in it, so I'd better make sure not to write them here.

Their new album is called *Scuttle 1000* and it is amazing. The first song to be released on the album is "Run the Pipes (Witches)," and here they are now on the sofa at Linden House!

Aggie Hoof: Hello, Silver Rats. I love you; you are so evil.

Big Ratty (Lydia Claw): We've decided to shed our evil image and it's all about being strong, good witches now.

Aggie Hoof: WHAT?!

Jam Jar (Annie Legs): Strong, good witches.

Aggie Hoof: WHAAAAT?!

Tails (Gemma Gray): Strong, good witches.

Aggie Hoof: But you have a song on your latest album called "EVIL IS THE BEST."

Big Ratty (Lydia Claw): That's actually a really deep song about being strong, good witches.

Aggie Hoof: GET OUT.

33

The Dolls

"DOLLS?!" Fluffanora cried. "It's always dolls! I suppose it's not that weird, is it? They're just giving Miss Flint their old dolls."

Tiga tipped the dolls out onto the sidewalk and picked one up. It was small with a puffy skirt and a sad look on its face.

"Yeah, maybe they're just doing a clearing out of Linden House. There are dolls in there . . . ," Tiga mumbled. She was getting fed up with this wild doll chase they seemed to be on. They were getting absolutely nowhere.

Fluffanora shook her head and plucked the doll out of Tiga's hand. She inspected its skirt and gasped.

"What is it?" Tiga and Fran cried at the same time.

Fluffanora shook her head. "It can't be . . . but it must be. It's so obvious what they're doing now!"

Tiga stared at her, unconvinced. "Really?"

"Look at the label on this skirt—it says 'Brew's,'" Fluffanora said pointedly.

"So?" said Tiga with a shrug.

Fluffanora stared at the doll in amazement. "Mom doesn't make skirts for dolls."

34

The Peggy Doll

Aggie Hoof was plonked on the sofa in the study with some frilly pants on her head. Felicity Bat was pacing back and forth, muttering to herself.

In her hand was a file of papers.

"What are you doing?" Aggie Hoof asked.

"These might just be the only papers in Sinkville that say who Tiga really is."

"WOW, cool, that's, wait—WHAT ARE YOU DOING?" Aggie Hoof squealed as Felicity Bat flicked her finger and set them on fire.

They fizzled in a little charcoaled pile on the floor and then vanished.

"Now I am the only one who can tell her who she is. I will have complete control over her," she said with a cackle.

Aggie Hoof cackled too and pulled a doll out from under the sofa cushions. It had wildly frizzy hair and big glasses.

"Poor little Piggy trapped in a doll," she said.

35

'Bye, Desperate Dolls

Tiga and Fluffanora stood outside Desperate Dolls. Fran hovered between them, her fists raised in the air.

Miss Flint hadn't opened the shop—presumably because her dress was still missing and she was very superstitious about the whole thing. She probably wasn't planning to open up the shop until she could figure out how to get it back.

Tiga scanned the dolls in the window and shook her head. "Do you think they are all shrunken witches?"

Fluffanora shrugged. "They can't all be witches. But I bet a lot of them are."

"How do we turn them back into normal-sized witches?" Tiga asked.

"It's probably one of those weird spells—the curse kind. You know, the ones from the olden days."

"Like the girl who falls asleep and a prince has to kiss her to wake her up?"

"Yes," said Fluffanora, "Ridiculous ones like that."

"Well, in that case, we might have to kiss all the dolls . . . ," Fran said.

Fluffanora wasn't paying attention; her eyes were fixed on the dolls in the window. She stepped forward, flicked her finger, and the window shattered.

"FLUFFANORA!" Tiga cried. "No need to break the window!"

Fluffanora flicked her finger again and sent the roof of the shop soaring off.

"Now you're just showing off," Tiga said as the four sides of the building fell over, flopping onto the sidewalk like limp leaves.

The three of them stood staring at the shelves full of dolls. Tiga ran up to one of the dolls, picked it up, and kissed it.

Nothing happened.

Nothing happened when she kissed the other 9,872 dolls either.

"Stop kissing the dolls! It's not working!" Fluffanora eventually shouted at Tiga and Fran, who had also been jumping on the dolls to see if that worked. "It's not working!"

"Well, what have you been doing this whole time?" Fran asked, an eyebrow raised.

"Nothing," said Fluffanora, holding a doll with elaborately braided hair behind her back.

"Why are you kissing dolls?" someone said.

Tiga spun around. Standing next to one of the shelves was Lizzie Beast!

"Lizzie! We think we've figured it out. Felicity Bat and Aggie Hoof have been turning witches into dolls! We think some of these dolls are witches."

Lizzie Beast held a doll in the air and stared at it for a moment. "Hello?" she whispered.

"We've been trying to figure out how to turn them back," Fluffanora explained.

Lizzie Beast shook the doll. "STOP BEING A DOLL!" she shouted.

Nothing happened.

"I think this is Darcy Dream, the editor of *Toad* magazine!" Fran cried as she prodded a very fashionable-looking doll.

"Really?" asked Tiga, picking up the doll and putting it in her skirt pocket. "In that case, let's take her with us. Maybe she can help us stop Aggie Hoof."

Fluffanora clapped her hands. "Right, and let's find Eddy Egg—I mean Peggy. Let's find Peggy so we can restore order in Ritzy City and stop Felicity Bat, and then we can figure out how to turn them back."

Tiga hadn't mentioned it, but not a single doll in Desperate Dolls looked like Peggy. She didn't want to say it out loud because that would only make it real.

"I don't think she's here," Fran said as she stole a hat from one of the dolls and plunked it on her beehive of hair.

Tiga bent down and picked up a bald doll.

"That's not a witch that's been turned into a doll!" Fran said. "I am p-o-s-i-t-ive."

"Fran!" Tiga said as she threw the bald doll back into the pile.

She spotted a doll wearing a little apron with a very tiny Clutterbucks logo on it. She thought that had to be the missing cake baker Mrs. Clutterbuck had mentioned. But there wasn't a single doll that looked like Peggy.

"Felicity Bat might be keeping Peggy somewhere safe, so no one can find her," Lizzie Beast suggested.

Lizzie Beast had a point. Peggy was the well-known ruler of Sinkville—a doll that looked like her might arouse suspicion. They couldn't just give her to Miss Flint to put on the shelves at Desperate Dolls. But where would they keep her?

"We need to figure out a way to get back into Linden House," said Tiga, "and NO! Fluffanora, before you suggest it, we are not going as designers from Shoeland again."

Fluffanora stomped her foot. "But it's so fun!"

"What if you were filming a TV show of some sort?" Lizzie Beast said. "We could use my mom's camera."

Lizzie Beast's mom was an infamous camera

operator in Brollywood, infamous because she had once sat on a fairy and squashed her.

Fran clutched her heart and fell to the ground. "Not the fairy flattener," she said.

Tiga ignored her. "An excellent idea, Lizzie Beast! Let's do that."

"I should direct! I know the most about show business!" Fran screeched.

"You can't be in it, Fran. They'll recognize you, even if you're in disguise. You'll have to hide in my hat," Tiga said.

Fran crossed her arms and a big clump of glittery dust fell from her skirt and hit the ground.

Fluffanora jumped up and down, "We can say it's a TV program about the new Shoeland fashions in Sinkville!"

Tiga sighed. Even though she knew it was genius.

36

The "TV Show"

"Today we stand in front of Linden House, the most important building in all of Sinkville, a place that has embraced the daring and downright gorgeous fashions of Shoeland."

Fluffanora was in her element. She was holding a microphone with BROLLYWOOD NEWS stamped on the front. Lizzie Beast had whipped up lots of spotlights, which were moving around above Fluffanora's head.

They were all in disguise. Fluffanora was wearing a tiny hat with her hair curled up inside it. She had added a beaded fringe to the rim so you could barely make out her face. Tiga was wearing a floppy hat (Fran was hiding inside it, in a huff because she wasn't allowed to

take part), and Lizzie Beast had big goggles on, plus the
camera in front of her face.

Witches began to flock and crowd around them.
Some started taking pictures. Some were even showing
off by doing the New Picture Spell rather than using a
camera.

All you had to do for the New Picture Spell was hold
a finger in the air and line it up with whatever you
wanted to take a picture of, and then say: "Snap it once

and snap it well! That is all there is to this spell. So, yeah . . . just take a photo of the thing, please."

That would be followed by a big flash and then the photo would come out of your mouth.

Tiga preferred using an actual camera.

"People say that the reason for these excellent fashions picking up pace in Sinkville can be credited to one witch, and one witch only," Fluffanora continued.

Tiga saw the living room curtain twitch.

"*Psst*, tell her to say it with more panache," Tiga heard Fran whisper from under her hat.

"She, the witch in question, lives inside this house with her best friend, Felicity Bat, the ruler of Sinkville. She has also taken on the demanding job of editor of *Toad* magazine, after the publication's actual editor went missing," Fluffanora stopped.

Tiga motioned at her to keep going.

"Some say she isn't really responsible for the new Shoeland fashions—"

"I AM RESPONSIBLE!" Aggie Hoof roared as the door flew open. She had shoes on her ears, again.

The crowd cheered. Aggie Hoof did a little spin.

"Oh, hello, Aggie Hoof. We are making a TV show for Brollywood News about . . . well, it's about how brilliant you are. Can we come in?" Fluffanora asked.

Aggie Hoof nodded madly, "Uh, obviously."

Once they were inside, they had to endure two hours of filming Aggie Hoof talking about how excellent she was.

"I'm actually working on a book," she boasted. "It's called *Horrible Shoes, Horrible People.* Do you know what it's about?"

Fluffanora sighed and shook her head. "Please enlighten us."

"It's about how you can tell exactly what someone is like from their shoes."

"Some people might think that's a bit superficial of you," Fluffanora couldn't resist saying. Tiga kicked her foot. "But, well, they would be . . . wrong," she said through gritted teeth.

"You know," said Aggie Hoof, "I'm also thinking of designing my own clothes. Mrs. Brew isn't very good, in my opinion, and her daughter, Fluffanora, doesn't know anything about fashion. She could have been friends with me but instead she chose to be friends with the disgustingly tattered Peggy Pigwiggle and this weird-looking girl from above the pipes. Who was wearing jeans."

Fluffanora slowly began rolling up her sleeves. Tiga looked on anxiously.

"You know," said Fluffanora fiercely, "maybe the Brew girl doesn't care what her friends are wearing. Maybe that's not the best way to pick friends."

"Oh no, it's the only way," Aggie Hoof said.

Tiga shot Fluffanora a look. She was worried Fluffanora had completely forgotten why they were there. And why they were there was to find Peggy and save her, not to pick a fight with Aggie Hoof.

Fluffanora stood up. "Well, excellent, you lovely, lovely, lo-ve-ly witch," she forced herself to say. "May we just wander around and take a few shots of the inside of the building?"

"Sure," said Aggie Hoof. She stood up and that's

when Tiga saw it, half hidden under the cushions on the sofa where Aggie Hoof had been sitting.

Tiga tried to catch Fluffanora's eye. "It's there," she tried to say out of the corner of her mouth. Lizzie Beast spotted what she was pointing at.

"Will you please be in the shots too, Ms. Hoof? They won't be the same without you," Lizzie Beast said urgently from behind the camera.

"Of course," Aggie Hoof said as she trotted out into the hallway.

As soon as they were gone, Tiga grabbed the doll. It was definitely Peggy.

"Peggy?" she whispered.

She was positive the doll's eyes moved. If only there was a spell to make it talk. She was sure there probably was one, but she was still learning about spells and had never seen . . . *wait*. THE FROG SPELL FLUFFANORA DID IN THE CAULDRON BOAT!

Tiga gently placed the Peggy doll down, pointed her finger, and said quickly, "Scream and sing and sometimes squeak. I give you, quiet thing, the power to SPEAK!"

She lowered her finger. Maybe it only worked on fro—

"Please tell me that TV show isn't real," the Peggy doll squeaked.

"PEGGY!" Tiga cried.

Fran shot out from under Tiga's hat. "It would have been a much better TV show if *I* had been in it."

37

The Lesson

"They put a doll on my doorstep," Peggy explained, although very slowly and very squeakily, as she was still a doll. "I was going to speak to Miss Flint about it. I had no idea who had put it there. Of course, now I know it was them, and Miss Flint was in on it. All I did was touch the doll and then I was sucked into it."

Tiga cuddled the tiny Peggy doll and placed it on the table. "There must be a way to turn you back . . . ," Tiga mumbled.

Peggy sort of smiled. "I knew you guys would find me. The Shoeland thing was hilarious; that kept me going, watching Aggie Hoof prance around the place with tights on her head and shoes on her ears."

Tiga laughed just as Aggie Hoof raced into the room and grabbed the Peggy doll.

Fran dived under Tiga's hat.

"This is mine," she snapped. "*MINE.*"

Felicity Bat glided into the room. "What's going on here?" she said, moving closer and closer to Fluffanora. Fluffanora took a step back.

"Oh, you thought you could fool me, did you?" Felicity Bat growled.

"These Brollywood News reporters aren't trying to fool anyone, Fel-Fel," Aggie Hoof said.

Felicity Bat pulled the hat off Tiga's head and threw it across the room. Fran went flying, smacked against the wall, and glittery dust exploded everywhere.

Aggie Hoof gasped. "How dare you!"

"You are both in terrible trouble," said a small voice.

It was the Peggy doll.

"Oh, well done, you did a spell to make her speak," Felicity Bat said with an amused cackle. "But you'll never figure out how to turn her back."

Tiga snatched the Peggy doll back and held it high above her head as Aggie Hoof jumped up and down trying to grab it.

"No one knows the spell, or how to reverse it," Felicity Bat went on. "It's my gran's secret invention. No one has ever figured it out and no one ever will."

She snatched the Peggy doll, ready to rip its head off.

Just then, the door flew open. "CURSES! CURSES EVERYWHERE!"

It was Miss Flint.

"My shop! It's gone! Destroyed! The roof is off, the window is smashed, the WALLS ARE GONE! CURSES! THE CURSES HAVE GOTTEN US!"

And then she ran out again. This time through the wall.

Felicity Bat stared dumbfounded at the Miss Flint–shaped hole in the wallpaper.

Fran shot some glittery dust in Felicity Bat's face and Tiga snatched the Peggy doll back.

"Oh, this is so boring," Felicity Bat said, wiping the glitter off her face.

Tiga felt like she had smoke coming out of her ears. "You are finished, Felicity Bat! I am going to tell everyone what you did and they are going to run you out of Linden House! Peggy will be Top Witch again and we will figure out how to turn her back into a witch."

Felicity Bat grinned, which wasn't what Tiga expected her to do at all. Felicity had lost. They had won. So why the grin?

"I suppose you've won, Tiga," began Felicity Bat. "There is nothing I could offer you. Well, I could tell you what your real surname is, and where you come from in Sinkville, and who your mother is. All I ask in return is for you to give me Peggy."

"You're bluffing!" Fran cried. "Her surname is Whicabim."

"It's a made-up name, Fran," Felicity Bat said, levitating above them. "Never in the history of Sinkville has there been a witch called Whicabim. That Miss Heks she used to live with above the pipes must have made it up, probably as a joke."

"I did think it was weird that when you jumbled up the letters in your name it spelled 'I am a big witch' . . . ," Fran mumbled.

Tiga could barely think—her mind was racing like Fran trying to out-fly Julie Jumbo Wings. She marched toward Felicity Bat. "And how do you know that there has never been a Whicabim?"

"Well?" squeaked the Peggy doll.

"We found it in the Mmmf," Aggie Hoof said proudly.

"The Mmmf?" Fluffanora scoffed. "No one can find anything in the Mmmf."

"Crispy did," Aggie Hoof said proudly.

Felicity Bat kicked her.

"Well, we will just ask Crispy to give us the information, then," Fran said.

"She just had to look for the word *Tiga* in documents," Felicity Bat said, waving her hand dismissively. "She didn't read the documents properly—she knows nothing."

"WHAT ARE YOU ALL TALKING ABOUT?!" Tiga cried.

"No witch called Whicabim has ever lived in Sinkville. You've been using the wrong surname this whole time, but I know what your real surname is." Felicity Bat took a seat on the sofa and smoothed out her skirt. "So, Tiga, I don't have all day, what will it be— the information or Peggy?"

"How will I know you're telling the truth?" Tiga asked.

"You won't," Felicity Bat said.

Tiga looked from Fluffanora to Fran to the Peggy doll and then to Felicity Bat, who was grinning a mad grin.

"And what's to stop me just going to the Mmmf and finding this information out for myself?"

"Well, the extreme dust in the place for one," Aggie Hoof said. "Also, Fel-Fel burned the file. The information's only in her brain now."

Tiga shot across the room and grabbed Felicity Bat's hair. She just levitated up high and shook Tiga off.

"Oh, hurry up and make your decision," Felicity Bat snapped.

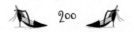

"Stop!" Fluffanora cried, looking from Tiga to the Peggy doll to Felicity Bat. "Tiga, think about this."

"I don't have to," Tiga said instantly. "I choose Peggy."

Fran covered her eyes.

"Okay, your real name is—WHAT? YOU CHOOSE PEGGY?!" Felicity Bat spluttered.

Tiga nodded and held the Peggy doll close to her chest. "I choose Peggy."

Felicity Bat floated in the air and blinked at her.

"Fel-Fel?" Aggie Hoof whispered. "That's not what you wanted her to say . . . is it?"

It wasn't what either of them had expected.

"You think everyone will behave as selfishly as you, Felicity!" Tiga said. "But we will not."

"I think there are occasions when I might . . . ," Fran mumbled to herself.

"Do you really think I would leave Peggy here, with you? I'm going to tell all of Sinkville what you did!" Tiga went on. "And all the other witches like the *Toad* editor, Darcy Dream." She pulled the Darcy Dream doll out of her pocket and bellowed the speaking spell.

"We are going to chase you out of town!" the Darcy Dream doll squeaked.

"EXACTLY," said Tiga.

Fran smiled proudly at her as Felicity Bat floated around in the air, utterly gobsmacked.

Fluffanora tapped Aggie Hoof on the shoulder. "Shoeland doesn't exist, by the way. I made it up."

Aggie Hoof stared at her closely. "No, you didn't."

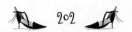

Fluffanora lifted the shoe off Aggie Hoof's ear and whispered, "I really did."

"WHAT?!" Aggie Hoof squealed. "But then that would make me . . . AN IDIOOOOOOTTTTT!"

Tiga marched to the door and flung it open. "WITCHES OF RITZY CITY! I AM TIGA AND I HAVE SOMETHING TO TELL YOU!"

Felicity Bat and Aggie Hoof looked at each other and then hurried out of Linden House, toward the winding road that snaked up and up and wrapped around Pearl Peak.

"Darcy Dream?" whispered a witch as she dropped a load of Brew's bags. "Is that you?"

"Meredith!" Darcy Dream squeaked from the doorway where she had flopped. "Take me back to *Toad* magazine headquarters this instant!"

TOAD MAGAZINE

It is me, Darcy Dream! I am back, although I am still a doll, so my assistant, Meredith, is very kindly writing this for me because my fingers are made of fabric and cannot grip a pen.

I was NOT playing hide-and-seek. I was turned into a doll by Aggie Hoof and her evil pal Felicity Bat.

As revenge, I have bewitched *Toad* magazine with a special spell just for Aggie Hoof. If she DARES to touch a copy of this magazine, it will shoot slime at her face and steal her shoes.

38

Celia Crayfish's Playroom

Fran straightened her beehive of hair. "Well, that's them gone!"

"I have a feeling Felicity Bat will be back again," Tiga groaned.

"Thank you so much, Tiga," the Peggy doll squeaked.

"We have to figure out how to turn you back," Tiga said.

"And we need to find out what your surname is," Peggy squeaked.

"AND we need to find Eddy Eggby," Fluffanora insisted. "Peggy, I think she was turned into a doll too, by Celia Crayfish all those years ago when Celia was only a baby."

"We could start with Celia Crayfish's playroom. It

still exists. I found it a couple of weeks before they turned me into a doll," Peggy squeaked. "It's hidden behind a little hatch under the stairs."

☆⭐☆

"She must be here! She just must!" Fluffanora shouted.

Tiga was beginning to worry Fluffanora might be disappointed as she squeezed herself through the dusty hatch and clawed her way along the cobweb-covered hallway.

It was really unlike her not to comment on the dust or cobwebs.

She turned to Tiga with cobwebs dangling from her eyelashes. "Isn't this BRILLIANT?!"

"Is it much farther?" Tiga asked the Peggy doll.

They followed the corridor as it curved left and right and got narrower and narrower. As they walked, the little lights that lined the walls flickered to life, illuminating portraits of Celia Crayfish as a young girl.

Celia Crayfish peeping out of a cauldron.

Celia Crayfish levitating in the air.

206

Celia Crayfish stomping on beetles.

There was a creaking sound and a couple of lights went out.

"I don't like this," Fran mumbled.

"I bet the Eddy Eggby doll is in her playroom," Fluffanora said as she ripped a portrait off the wall and forged on ahead. "How far is this playroom, anyway? Ah! Here's the door."

She kicked it with her sparkly shoe and sent it flying off its hinges, revealing, well, not a playroom, that was for sure.

Tiga gasped.

"That," said Fran, pointing a tiny finger at what lay beyond the door, "is a forest."

39

Slime

Felicity Bat raised an eyebrow. "Why are you covered in slime and not wearing any shoes?"

Aggie Hoof dropped her *Toad* magazine and SCREAMED.

Into the Forest...

The air in the forest was cool, almost frosty, and the trees seemed to whisper nothing but bad things.

"HANDS UP, WHO WANTS TO GO BACK NOW?" Fran bellowed, stretching an arm in the air.

"It's over there," Peggy said, peeking out of Tiga's pocket. But because she was a doll, she couldn't point or nod or anything like that.

"There?" asked Tiga, pointing Peggy at a line of crooked trees.

"No, it's—" Peggy began.

"Here?" Tiga asked, pointing her toward another line of crooked trees.

"I'VE FOUND IT!" Fluffanora shouted.

Tiga raced over to where she was hunched, next to a

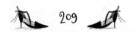

tall and spindly tree. Carved into the trunk were the initials C.C. and around it was a ring of terrifying-looking stone dolls.

Tiga tapped one of the stone dolls with her foot and it sank slowly into the ground, followed by the one next to it, and the one next to that.

Fran covered her eyes.

"Pretty elaborate entrance for a playroom," Tiga mumbled.

The C.C. on the trunk glowed brightly and then *BANG!* The tree split in two, opening up to reveal a slide. A black shimmering liquid sploshed down it, spiraling down and down until there was no light to see if it went any farther.

Fluffanora threw her hat across the forest like a Frisbee and leapt onto it. Within less than a second she had shot off down the slide and vanished completely.

"FLUFFANORA!" Tiga yelled as she tucked the Peggy doll into her skirt and tore off after her.

Fran stood whistling by the tree for a moment and then felt really guilty.

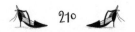

"I'M COMING, TIGA! FABULOUS FRAN IS ON HER WAY!"

As the water slide swirled its last swirl, Tiga slipped from the end of it and felt herself free-falling through the darkness.

She could just make out a small light, getting brighter as she hurtled closer toward it.

"Fran!" she cried as the fairy soared really close to her, with a very bright finger.

"Well, this is very odd," Fran said, wagging her glowing finger around to reveal lots of floating toy boxes engraved with doodles of dolls.

Tiga somersaulted through the air.

"Oh look, ground!" Fran shouted as Tiga landed with a thump on top of Fluffanora, who shoved her off, leapt to her feet, and started rummaging in the hundreds of toy boxes that filled the room.

"Eddy Eggby's got to be here, Tiga!"

Tiga slowly uncrumpled herself and scanned the room. Unlike the cobwebbed corridor, the dusty hatch, and the creepy forest, the room was perfect, like it was brand-new. An ornate black toy train blew its horn as it tore around a track that circled above their heads.

"It's an exact replica of the Sinkville Express," Peggy squeaked.

"The Sinkville Express?" Tiga asked. "I've never seen it."

"It hasn't been in the sky for years," Fluffanora

explained. "Celia Crayfish took it down. It used to connect all the cities in Sinkville."

She marched to the corner of the room, grabbed a broom, and soared up to the toy boxes floating in the darkness above them. When she opened one, it was empty. She flew over to one of the trunks and opened that too. Again, nothing.

"Where are all the dolls?" Fluffanora said crossly as she zoomed around in the air.

Tiga and Peggy got to work on the things that were scattered across the ground—mostly cauldrons, cuddly frog toys, and board games. Tiga really liked the look of one game called BROOMSTICK BOOM, but there wasn't any time to try it.

Fran sat back in the air and watched, occasionally flicking her finger and lifting things for the others if they needed it. She also sneakily tried to rearrange Tiga's hair, which she had decided was a bit messy.

"Stop that!" Tiga said as she felt her hair ruffling and rearranging itself into a large beehive. "FRAN!"

"You would look wonderful with a beehive!"

Peggy giggled. Tiga turned to glare at Fran and that's when she spotted it. Propped up against the wall behind Fran was a painting. A painting of Celia Crayfish. She must have been about six or seven years old in it. She was sporting a twisted grin and clutching a small doll wearing a hat with a huge pom-pom . . .

"Fluffanora?" Tiga said.

Peggy spotted what Tiga was looking at. "Fluffanora . . . ," she squeaked.

"Oh, what's the point in having a load of floating old trunks and cupboards if you don't keep the thing I'm looking for in them, for FROGS' SAKE?!" she shouted, kicking one of the cupboards and falling off her broom.

She landed with a thud next to Peggy and Tiga. "What are you two staring at—oh, my frogbags, it's EDDY EGGBY BUT SHE'S A DOLL!!!"

Pom-pom Hat

There was no mistaking that the little doll in Celia Crayfish's claws was the fantastically fashionable Eddy Eggby.

But where was she now?

It had been weeks since they had fallen into Celia Crayfish's old playroom and found the very convincing evidence that Eddy Eggby had been turned into a doll. But they still hadn't tracked her down.

Fran had even mentioned the incident on her TV show, *Cooking for Tiny People*, which she assured Tiga was watched by millions. But still not a single witch or fairy had come forward.

Peggy was still a doll and Miss Flint's shop had been closed down (because Fluffanora had taken the roof off it, and all the sides, so someone had just hung a CLOSED sign on the only shelf that remained standing). No one had seen Miss Flint for days, but everyone knew she would be in big trouble when she was found.

Fluffanora had rebranded Linden House "Dolls HQ" and was demanding to stay there, so Mrs. Brew had joined them, along with about fifty Brew's shop witches, who were all buzzing around the place helping out with the mission to find Eddy Eggby. All the Brew's witches had come dressed as weird-looking witch detectives, with froggy hats and slick black jumpsuits should they need to chase or attack.

Their time to attack did eventually come, one quiet night when the grand old clock in the corridor coughed nine and there was a massive bang downstairs.

"BACK OFF, YOU RITZY CITY FOOLS!" a witch bellowed.

Tiga crept down the stairs. In the dim light of the hallway she could make out a circle of Brew's witches around a tall dark figure standing in the dim light.

"Miss Flint!" Tiga cried, racing down the stairs two at a time, clutching the Peggy doll. Fluffanora was behind her (in an eye mask—she had been sleeping). When she got to the bottom of the stairs she ran straight into a statue. Fran was behind her (also in an eye mask). She also banged into the statue.

"What are you doing here, Miss Flint?" Tiga asked, stepping past the little Brew's witches. "You're in a lot of trouble."

One of the lanterns bobbing up and down outside the window was gently casting a soft glow down the corridor and onto Miss Flint's old face. She looked like she had never looked before. She didn't look angry. She didn't look furious. She looked really, really sad.

"Before I start," she said, clearing her throat. "I don't like them witches from Ritzy City. None of you. But I would never hurt a fly. I did once hurt a fly, so that's a lie. But I did it by accident. Sat on it."

"ARE YOU SURE IT WASN'T A FAIRY?!" Fran asked, her nostrils flared.

"It was a fly. Because I sat on it up there in the world above the pipes," Miss Flint said.

Tiga took a step forward. "Were you terrorizing children up there?"

Miss Flint shook her head madly. "No, no. I told you, I would never hurt a fly, apart from that one I sat on."

"Well, what were you doing up there?" Peggy asked.

Miss Flint stepped closer to them. "I was delivering dolls; Celia Crayfish asked me to take them up there. But I didn't know they were cursed witches! I thought they were dolls. Some of them looked like witches I had seen before, but I just thought they were dolls modeled on them! I didn't know they were real witches! Everyone's been talking about what Felicity Bat did to Peggy and those other witches, but I promise I didn't know. I didn't."

Peggy, Tiga, and Fluffanora all gasped.

"So . . . ," Fluffanora said. "Let me get this straight. You didn't know that many of the dolls in your doll shop could be cursed witches?"

Miss Flint shook her head.

"And, at the request of Celia Crayfish, you took some of those dolls up to the world above the pipes and left them there?" Tiga asked.

Miss Flint nodded.

"I hate to say sorry to Ritzy City witches, but I am. I'm so sorry. I had no idea. When I was little I dreamed of opening my own shop. I wanted to fix things. There were so many dolls lying around the place that no one took the time to help. I wanted to be the one that helped. I worked hard at that old sandwich shop, Nibblers, and got enough sinkels together to buy my very own shop, and I was proud of that place. And now it's gone."

Tiga looked at Fluffanora, who was guiltily looking at her finger.

"The curses got it," Miss Flint continued. "The walls fell off and everything."

Tiga kept looking at Fluffanora. She expected her to say, "Oh, sorry, it wasn't the curses, it was actually me." But she just mumbled, "Curses are terrible things . . ."

Tiga was about to say something, but then she remembered the photo! She hurried to the study, grabbed it, and came sliding back into the hallway. "If that is true, then how do you explain this?"

She held the picture of Eddy Eggby on Ritzy Avenue under Miss Flint's pointy nose.

"There, right there, you can very clearly see you slipping a doll into Eddy Eggby's bag, RIGHT BEFORE she went to see Celia Crayfish and was turned into a doll."

Miss Flint gasped. "It was bad to slip the doll in her bag, but I just wanted to give the child a doll! Eddy Eggby was going on about bringing her a

Clutterbucks drinks machine—what's a baby going to do with that?!"

"So you just slipped it in her bag?" Tiga asked. "As a gift?"

Miss Flint nodded. "Eddy Eggby must have given the doll to Celia Crayfish and maybe that's how she got the idea to come up with the spell. Maybe she wanted to keep Eddy Eggby forever, so by shrinking her and turning her into her doll, she could!"

"So where is the Eddy doll now?" Fluffanora asked.

"London," said Miss Flint without hesitation. "I took it to London."

To London!

"This is such an excellent excuse to wear jeans!" Fluffanora said as she threw a pair at Tiga.

Tiga stuffed them in her bag and took off her hat.

"Should we wear hats? Not many people wear hats above the pipes, especially not ones that are pointy and witchlike, which these certainly will be after we've been sucked up the pipes," she rambled.

"But we're witches! We should wear our hats!" Fluffanora said.

"Agreed," squeaked Peggy.

Tiga rolled her eyes. "Very subtle. Why don't we just carry a massive spell book and a cat as well?!"

Fluffanora held up a spell book and Fuzzscrumple the scraggly cat. "So weird you just said that. I thought

we should bring a spell book, just in case, and I spoke to Miss Flint and she said Fuzzscrumple knows exactly where to go in London."

☆⭐☆

Fluffanora, one doll, one fairy, one cat, and one worried Tiga stared at a very complicated map of all the pipes.

"What's Tokyo?" Fluffanora asked.

"It's a city in Japan," Tiga said.

Peggy pointed at a pipe that said NEW YORK. "Is it very new?" she asked.

Tiga tapped the London pipe. "This is the one we need . . . I wonder where it takes you in London. According to this, the pipe is just above us, dangling over the roof of Linden House."

Fluffanora wiggled with excitement as she climbed the stairs to the attic, clambered out onto the roof, and stared up at the large leaking pipe above their heads.

"Ready?" Tiga said.

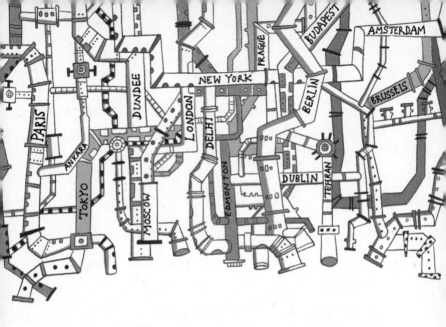

Fluffanora adjusted the strap of her cool mirrored silver bag. "Ready," she said.

Fran nodded. They each raised an arm in the air (Tiga had to raise Peggy's limp little doll arm), and *WHOOSH*! Off they went to London town.

43

Bedford Square

They had landed on a quiet, treelined street.

"Bedford Square," Tiga said, peering at the street sign. "I have no idea where we are."

A girl on a pretty yellow bike pedaled past.

Fluffanora whipped out her notebook and sketched her. "She's wearing a little wrap dress," she mumbled. She looked up and saw Tiga staring at her. "I could be the next Eddy Eggby!"

"Where do we go, Fuzzscrumple?" Tiga asked as a group of people walked past. Tiga heard one of the women say, "Look at those little girls dressed as witches."

It was nowhere near Halloween. It was time to get out of there.

Fuzzscrumple took a left and then a right and made

his way all the way to the end of the road, stopped, and then let out a weird scream of a meow. Tiga looked around nervously, then up at the building.

The windows were so dusty you could barely see inside, and the cobwebs that hung above the door swayed slowly in the breeze.

DELIA'S DOLLS was scrawled on a rusty old sign outside.

Great, Tiga thought. *Another creepy doll shop.*

Delia's Dolls

"Well, I'll be darned by a frog in a boat made of feathers. It's a bunch of Ritzy City witches!" cried the woman behind the counter. She looked a lot like Miss Flint, only smaller and with wildly curly hair. She had a raspy voice and long spindly fingers tipped with clawlike nails painted with gray, glittery polish.

Her pale gray eyes fixed on Tiga. "I'm Delia Drizzle, and you are?"

"Tiga. This is Fluffanora, and Fran."

Fuzzscrumple stuck a claw into Tiga's toe. "And this is Fuzzscrumple," she said through gritted teeth.

"Old Miss Flint's cat!" Delia Drizzle said with a cackle.

"Are you one of the Big Exit witches?" Fluffanora

asked. They had all heard about the witches who had left for a life above the pipes during the Big Exit. Tiga knew Fluffanora was asking because it was believed the Big Exit witches were really terrible and probably went to live above the pipes so they could terrorize children.

Delia Drizzle shook her head. "Oh no! I'm not one of those angry sorts. I've got nothing against Ritzy City or any of Sinkville. I travel back below the pipes often. I have a little apartment in Ritzy City. My job is to keep this shop as a lookout—a link from our world down there to this world up here. It's also handy for Miss Flint—she has so many dolls, it's good to ship the unwanted ones up here, for me to fix 'em up and sell 'em on."

"So you had no idea that many of the dolls she's been sending might be witches that have been cursed?" the Peggy doll squeaked.

Delia Drizzle nearly shot through the roof!

"WHAT?! Talking dolls? Witches?! I don't believe it. Never!"

Tiga nodded. "Celia Crayfish came up with a spell

icity Bat

ted with

e.

oupe and

said Delia

ile to reach

to be a bit

ared up and

d her. "How

and how do

have similar

ained.

back," Peggy

that's not very

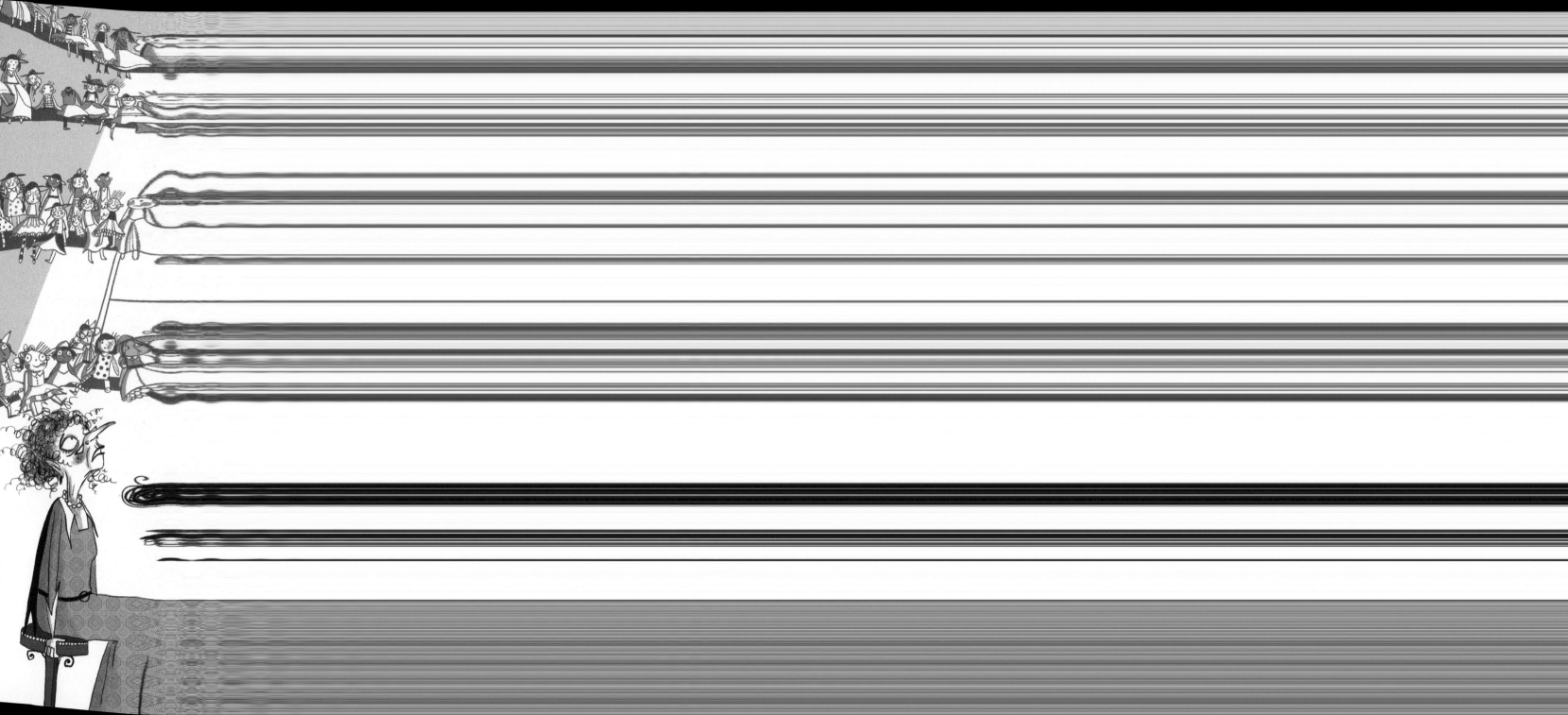

years ago to turn witches into dolls, and Felicity Bat knows it and started doing it again. She started with Peggy."

Tiga held the Peggy doll up to Delia Drizzle.

"But I heard Peggy joined a fairy dance troupe and put some rats in charge until she got back," said Delia Drizzle.

Tiga laughed. "That's not quite right."

"Ah," said Delia Drizzle. "News takes a while to reach me up here, and when it does, it tends to be a bit wrong."

She took a seat on a rickety stool and stared up and up at the hundreds of shelves of dolls around her. "How do we know which ones are really witches, and how do we turn them back?"

"They usually resemble the witch—have similar features, hair, the same clothes," Tiga explained.

"We don't know how to turn them back," Peggy squeaked.

Delia Drizzle frowned at her. "Well, that's not very good for you, is it?"

"We'll figure it out," Tiga muttered.

"Fluffanora and Tiga have gotten NOWHERE with their investigation," Fran said, completely butting in. "It is actually amazing how little success they have had. Every time they get somewhere, something sets them back to square one! I'm surprised they haven't given up already!"

She turned to see Tiga and Fluffanora, and Fuzzscrumple, glaring at her.

"What? Oh, don't make faces at me," Fran said crossly. "Look at Peggy; she's not making a face."

"That's because my face is currently made of some sort of felt," the Peggy doll squeaked.

Fluffanora stepped forward. "We're looking for one doll in particular. A doll with a pom-pom hat."

Delia Drizzle thought for a moment. "You know, it's funny, you aren't the first witches to ask me that. Quite a long time ago, a young woman came into my shop and asked me the very same thing. She was behaving very suspiciously—all nervous and shifty."

"And did you know the doll she meant?" Fluffanora asked eagerly.

Delia Drizzle nodded. "Oh yes. I gave it to her."

Tiga and Fluffanora slumped over the counter and sighed. Of course the doll wouldn't be there! That would be just their luck.

"Just your luck!" Fran said with a chuckle, before adding, ". . . Sorry."

"Funny thing was, though," Delia Drizzle said as she reached under the counter, "not long after I gave it to the witch, Miss Flint returned it to me!"

Tiga looked up and there, right in her face, was a huge pom-pom. Delia Drizzle wiggled it. "This the one?"

"EDDY EGGBY!" Fluffanora cried.

NAPA

After Delia Drizzle handed over the doll, they—three witches, one fairy, two dolls, and one bedraggled cat—sat down for some tea.

Tiga did the honors and finally, for the first time in one hundred years, Eddy Eggby could speak.

She told them hilarious stories from her years as a doll. Like the time an entire shelf of dolls had fallen on Delia Drizzle, or the time Miss Flint hadn't realized the door to the shop was closed and had walked right into it. But generally, being a doll for a hundred years sounded pretty boring.

"Who came to get you from Delia's shop all those years ago?" Tiga asked.

"It's very strange," squeaked the Eddy Eggby doll, at

such a high pitch that Fuzzscrumple winced. "You remind me so much of her. It is uncanny really. Gretal Green was her name. She worked for NAPA."

"NAPA?" Tiga asked.

"Yes, the National Above the Pipes Association. NAPA," the Eddy Eggby doll squeaked. "They study the world above the pipes. NAPA headquarters was based in Silver City."

"Silver City?" Tiga asked. "That's one of the cities that is now empty after the Big Exit, isn't it?"

Delia Drizzle nodded. "I was one of NAPA's Watcher Witches, reporting on things happening above the pipes."

"Gretal Green was an inventor at NAPA. She invented many great things over the years," Eddy Eggby squeaked away. "She was in charge of many top-secret operations, mostly schemes to protect children above the pipes. She was very concerned for them. Certain bad witches—probably influenced by the evil Celia Crayfish—became very interested in terrorizing the children above the pipes. Below the pipes, young witch children have magic;

an old witch is no match for them. But above the pipes, children are helpless when faced with an evil witch. Gretal Green was the one who lined the pipes with a spell to make bad witches particularly tattered. It was very clever, really. The worse the witch, the more damage the pipes do. Whereas if you are good, you usually just get covered in slime and a tiny bit tattered. And the spell made sure the witches' clothes would be bewitched to be only ever black or gray above the pipes. That way, children above the pipes would be able to recognize a witch a mile off."

"So why did she come and get you?" Fluffanora asked.

The Eddy Eggby doll blinked, inhaled a lot of air, and squeaked. "She was a fan. She had read a lot about my fashion findings and was curious as to where I had disappeared to. She began to investigate my disappearance and sent over fifty witches on missions to look for me in the queen's bathroom. Nothing," she squeaked. "So she ruled out that theory."

"Once she figured out you were a doll, why didn't she tell everyone?" Tiga asked.

"She was going to—she was gathering as much evidence as possible," Eddy Eggby squeaked.

"Why didn't she tell Delia Drizzle some of the dolls might be witches?" Fluffanora asked.

"She thought Delia Drizzle might be in on it. So she came in and pretended she just needed a doll for her little daughter."

"I WASN'T IN ON IT," Delia Drizzle scoffed, flinging her arm in the air and sending tea flying. Tiga flicked her finger and the stream of tea changed direction and went soaring back into her cup.

"I spent three lovely weeks sitting on the desk at NAPA," Eddy continued. "I watched her work on her inventions and play with Tiga."

Tiga and Fluffanora both choked on their tea and spat it out, sending a mist of tea spit soaring through the air and smack-dab into Fran. Who dropped to the ground in shock.

"Tiga?" the Peggy doll squeaked.

"Yes, Tiga," the Eddy Eggby doll squeaked back.

"I'm Tiga," Tiga said.

 236

Delia Drizzle gasped. "I thought she looked familiar! She looks just like her!"

"How old are you?" the Eddy Eggby doll squeaked.

"Nine and a bit," Tiga said.

"It fits! You are Tiga Green; you must be!" Fluffanora squealed, leaping to her feet and jumping up and down.

Tiga's heart was beating so fast, it was making more noise than Fran on an episode of *Cooking for Tiny People*. She could almost hear it in her eyeballs.

"So . . . what happened to Gretal Green?" Tiga dared to ask, although she was almost sure she didn't want to know. After all, Eddy Eggby had been returned to Delia's Dolls. Something must have gone wrong.

"Do you know about the Big Exit?" Eddy Eggby squeaked.

Everyone nodded.

"It's when a bunch of evil witches left to live above the pipes and they took their houses and all the color with them," Tiga said. She'd heard it a million times.

"When that happened," Eddy Eggby explained, through her little doll lips, "the bad witches came to see Gretal Green. They wanted to know how to move their houses above the pipes and how to stop what the pipes did to witches. They didn't want to stand out and look like witches. Of course, it's impossible to change what the pipes do to witches—it's built into the pipes themselves. So they thought of something else. They wanted to know how to steal the color. Children and adults alike, above the pipes, had gotten so used to thinking of witches in tattered black clothes with warty faces and pointy noses. If they couldn't change what the pipes did to them, they thought if they at least took the color, maybe people wouldn't suspect they were witches. A warty witch in, say, luminous yellow or a friendly orange doesn't look much like a witch at all."

"And Gretal Green said no to them, I suppose," Tiga mumbled. "She wanted to protect the children above the pipes."

The Eddy Eggby doll blinked. "Exactly. And those witches weren't pleased. They took her away—and her daughter too. And they gave me back to that Miss Flint! Who sewed new feet on me and sent me all the way back up here again!"

"Well, surely people have been looking for Gretal?" Tiga said.

Delia Drizzle shook her head. "Many people suspected the witches of NAPA had something to do with the Big Exit. And, of course, everyone in Silver City vanished. All the witches left behind just assumed the other witches were evil and had gone to live a life above the pipes."

"But Gretal Green wasn't evil; she didn't want to leave Silver City!" Tiga cried.

"She certainly wasn't evil," Eddy Eggby said.

"Well then, we have to find Gretal Green," the Peggy doll squeaked. "We'll search for her. We will search every inch of Sinkville from high on Pearl Peak to every spindly stilt in Silver City. We *will* find her."

Tiga stared into Peggy's kind plastic eyes and smiled.

Party!

In Ritzy City everyone was partying because Peggy was back!

Sort of. She was still a doll, but she was *technically* back!

Tiga held one plastic hand and Fluffanora held the other, and they swung the little Peggy doll back and forth to the sound of the Silver Rats playing on the stage outside Linden House. Fran flew above their heads.

"GENUINE HATS WOT GOT STUCK IN THE PIPES!"

The old witch with the cart of disgusting hats wheeled her way past them.

"Wait," Tiga said to Fluffanora. She'd had a brilliant idea! "The cart witch—she says she knows everything.

Maybe she'll know how to turn the dolls back into witches!"

"That's true," said the cart witch. "GENUINE HATS!"

"But she was wrong about the prophecy," said Fluffanora. "Remember, all that:

> *'An elegant witch will rule this land,*
> *and that bossy one will lend a hand.*

Witch sisters, maybe, but not the same.
One is dear.
The other? A PAIN.
And, much like the tales of times gone by,
They will find a sweet apple and . . . My oh my, is
that the time? I'd better go.'

For a start, Peggy is not being helped by someone who
is a pain."

Tiga raised an eyebrow.

"I am not a pain, before you say anything," Fluffanora
said.

"AND DON'T LOOK AT ME, TIGA GREEN,"
Fran said, wagging her finger.

"And," Fluffanora went on, "is Peggy elegant? If she
wasn't a doll right now, she'd be doing her arms-
everywhere dancing."

"Hey!" the Peggy doll squeaked.

Fluffanora grinned. "And I don't even know what
that apple bit means."

"You will . . . soon," the cart witch said quietly. So

quietly, only Fran heard. She narrowed her eyes at the cart witch, who just stared blankly ahead.

"Well then, this is a test, isn't it?" Tiga handed the cart witch the Peggy doll. "If she does know everything, she'll be able to turn her back."

The cart witch handed the Peggy doll back to Tiga.

"Aha! See," Fluffanora said. "She doesn't know."

The cart witch pointed at the doll. "Hold it by the hair and swing it around your head three times."

"Don't," squeaked the Peggy doll.

"And then blow in its face once," she added, before disappearing with a bang.

Gretal Green

And that's how Peggy, Eddy Eggby, Darcy Dream, and all the other witches who had been turned into dolls were changed back again.

Eddy Eggby went straight to the Coves, and Lily Cranberry nearly fainted when she saw her! Her best friend was back, and there was lots of cake to eat and partying to be done.

Back in Ritzy City the party raged on, and Tiga and Peggy danced up and down the streets cheering as Peggy leapt around doing her famous "dancing."

Tiga smiled and looked around her. Fran was clapping above Peggy's head and shooting glittery dust into the air. She couldn't see Fluffanora anywhere— maybe she had gotten fed up with the dancing; that would be quite Fluffanora . . . She stared past the crowds, off down the road toward the edge of Ritzy City where the twinkling lights stopped and darkness took over. Somewhere out there, in the depths of Sinkville, was Gretal Green. Tiga was sure of it.

"Tiga," Mrs. Brew asked as she walked fast through the crowd toward her, "could you come with me for a moment?"

"CAN I COME TOO BECAUSE I LOVE YOU?" Fran roared in Mrs. Brew's face.

Mrs. Brew nodded and rubbed her ear.

She guided them toward Brew's, slotted a little key in the door, and ushered them quickly inside. Shop witches in puffy little Brew's skirts were darting about the place restocking the shelves for the next day.

Mrs. Brew whistled and the huge chandelier that hung above them glided down.

"Hop on," she said.

Tiga stared at her in amazement. "Are we going to your studio?"

Mrs. Brew nodded.

Fran clutched her heart and fell to the ground.

No one ever got to see inside Mrs. Brew's studio. Not even Fluffanora.

The three of them clambered onto the chandelier and Mrs. Brew whistled again, sending the thing shooting up into the air. They soared fast past all the floors, up and up toward the shimmering black roof, which opened as they approached, and straight through they went.

"Excuse the mess," Mrs. Brew said as the chandelier came to a halt.

Tiga and Fran stared gobsmacked at the room. It was filled to bursting with beautiful fabrics. Pencils moved by magic, sketching gorgeous designs on floating bits of paper. Shoes marched by themselves across the room, changing patterns as they went. At the end of the long, narrow room sat a desk covered in paintbrushes and pencils and stacks of *Toad* magazines.

Mrs. Brew jumped off the chandelier, over the line of shoes making their way around the room, and reached behind the desk.

"You know, when Fluffanora told me about Gretal Green, I remembered something from a long time ago," Mrs. Brew shouted from behind her desk. "It . . . must be somewhere . . . right . . . here."

She held up a tiny black tape. "We used to record things on these. This is from my days as a student in Silver City. They did a documentary about the place and interviewed me for it. I was very proud to be on it."

"I hope they made the whole thing about you, because you are *amazing*," Fran oozed.

Mrs. Brew smiled. "Take a seat," she said to Tiga and Fran as two comfy little armchairs appeared with a bang.

She placed the tape in a small black device on her desk and a grainy, old, gray image appeared on the wall.

"That's Silver City, you see. Most of the buildings are on those stilts. It's very beautiful, really."

Tiga stared at it as the image began to move.

SILVER CITY~A PLACE OF WONDER & WONDERFUL WITCHES appeared on the screen.

It did all seem quite familiar to Tiga . . .

248

A voice began to talk. "This is Silver City, the second-largest city in Sinkville. Ritzy City, the capital of Sinkville, is, of course, the largest. But we feel we are the greatest."

"It looks really cool," said Tiga as she watched lots of witches march along silver platforms held in place by tall and spindly silver stilts. "Is Silver City definitely completely empty now?"

Mrs. Brew frowned. "It is. Every witch in the place left during the Big Exit. I can't believe every witch in the city was evil, it just can't be right, but that's what everyone believes."

"Here is our very successful design school, the Silver School of Art and Design," the presenter went on. "And here we have Georgia Brew, a very promising young designer."

They showed a much younger Mrs. Brew sketching some dresses. Her hair was short and spiky and she was wearing a floaty skirt with a huge holey sweater that was cinched in at the waist with a big sparkly belt.

"You look so cool!" Tiga said as Mrs. Brew blushed.

"And here in the NAPA headquarters we have another promising young witch, Gretal Green, who is working on some very secret inventions."

There was a large bang and the small young woman on the screen screeched and yelled, "FROGTRUMPETS!"

She straightened up her small hat and smiled at the screen. She looked a bit nervous, glanced away and looked back at the screen, moving closer to it this time.

Tiga gasped.

"I knew I recognized the name," Mrs. Brew said. "That's her, Tiga."

Tiga felt her eyes stinging. She looked away from Mrs. Brew so she wouldn't see she was teary, but Fran was already right in front of her waving a massive hankie.

"You have a good cry, my dear! Don't you worry!"

"Fraaaan," Tiga grumbled, taking the hankie and hiding her face with it. "Did you know her?" she asked.

Mrs. Brew shook her head. "No, I just remembered her because of this documentary. I don't think I ever met her."

When Tiga peeked back at the screen, she saw Gretal Green laughing as she pointed at a tank full of slugs.

"We're working to enhance the slugs' brain capacity, so they can go up above the pipes and collect information for us," she said, her voice wobbling nervously. "The problem is finding a way to extract the information once they have collected it, as I don't think we are ever going to get the slugs to talk."

"She has such a nice voice!" Tiga said.

"You have a slug, Tiga . . . ," Mrs. Brew said.

"The star of *Toe Pinchers*, apparently," Fran said sarcastically.

Mrs. Brew raised an eyebrow. "*Toe Pinchers?* Is that the horror film I've seen posters for?"

Fran tutted.

Tiga leapt to her feet and pointed at the screen. "The slug has always been in my shed! Maybe she's one of my mom's slugs! Maybe she has important information stored in her extra-clever brain!"

Mrs. Brew nodded. "Maybe . . ."

252

The documentary cut to a picture of a young girl with a load of frogs clinging to her hair.

"This is Olga Flopp. She has frogs permanently stuck to her head," the documentary narrator explained. "No one is quite sure why."

And then it clipped to a gloriously glossy, fast-flowing silver river.

"Is that in the city?" Tiga asked.

Mrs. Brew nodded. "Sort of. It's the way in. It swirls around the city—you have to ride it all the way around."

"That's where I'm going to go tomorrow. Me and Peggy . . . and Fluffanora, if we can convince her," Tiga rambled. "That's where we need to start the search. We're going to find Gretal Green!"

"Speaking of Fluffanora," said Mrs. Brew. "Where is she? I haven't seen her all day."

"She said something about going to the Docks," said Fran, flying through the air and plonking herself in one of the self-walking shoes. She lay back in it like it was a lawn chair. "Aaah, this is the life," she said.

"The Docks?" Tiga and Mrs. Brew said at the same time.

"Yes, the Docks," said Fran.

Mrs. Brew walked up to Fran. "What reason would she have to go there?"

Fran shrugged. "She definitely said the Docks."

"I might go check on her . . . ," Mrs. Brew mumbled.

"I'll come too," Tiga said.

48

Desperate Dolls, Again

When they pulled up in the Docks in Mrs. Brew's car, Ratty Ann, it was very quiet.

Everyone was in Ritzy, partying. But there was a faint banging sound, and an occasional clang of metal.

"I think you could make the sign sparkly," they heard Fluffanora say. "No harm in a bit of sparkle here and there."

"Not my style, really," said Miss Flint. "But we could put some sparkle along the edge of the desk there, maybe?"

Fluffanora was on her tiptoes on a stool, hanging some lovely silky curtains in a brand-new and brilliant-looking Desperate Dolls.

"And we have lots of spare little bits of fabric and things that Mom could give you to make dresses for the dolls," Fluffanora said, noticing the visitors. "Couldn't we, Mom?"

Mrs. Brew nodded slowly as she and Tiga stood surveying the scene, completely astonished.

"And maybe you could send some of your dolls to our shop and we could have a little 'Desperate Dolls' stall in there so people can buy your dolls there too," Fluffanora prattled on.

Miss Flint beamed and shyly nodded her head. "A stall in Brew's, well, that would really be something . . . And of course it's near Cakes, Pies, and That's About It Really."

Fluffanora nodded. "You could come and eat the tarts."

Miss Flint's cheeks darkened a little with embarrassment. "Yes . . . I've never tried them."

"Come on, you two!" Tiga called to Fluffanora and Miss Flint. "This can wait; you're missing an excellent party in Ritzy City!"

49

That Apple

Everyone in Ritzy City danced for hours that night to the sound of the Silver Rats.

But as they did, high above them in one of the pipes, a wrinkled old hand slid slowly into view.

Its crooked and crinkled fingers unfurled to reveal an apple colored the brightest of greens.

Slowly it fell, down and down, until it landed with a quiet thud among the dancing crowds. Their laughter and singing drowned out the evil cackles that echoed in the pipes above them.

No one in Ritzy City would notice the apple until morning.

When it was much too late.